To Brenda & Terry

With best Wishes.

2014

***Also by J. Robert DiFulgo*:**

The Invisible Moon

In progress: Earth's Final Sun and Moon

TITANIC'S RESURRECTED SECRET—HEW

J. Robert DiFulgo

iUniverse LLC
Bloomington

TITANIC'S RESURRECTED SECRET—HEW

iUniverse books may be ordered through booksellers or by contacting:

iUniverse LLC
1663 Liberty Drive
Bloomington, IN 47403
www.iuniverse.com
1-800-Authors (1-800-288-4677)

ISBN: 978-1-4917-2270-1 (sc)
ISBN: 978-1-4917-2269-5 (hc)
ISBN: 978-1-4917-2268-8 (e)

Library of Congress Control Number: 2014901317

Printed in the United States of America.

iUniverse rev. date: 05/12/2014

For Elena, my mother,

and

Anne

In Memoriam

Michael Rudd

(1942–2008)

Read not to contradict and confute; nor to believe and take for granted; nor to find talk and discourse, but to weigh and consider.
—Francis Bacon, "Of Studies," *Essaies* of 1597

No matter how important a book or manuscript may be, I only want those that interest me.
—Harry Elkins Widener

Harry Elkins Widener, AD 1907, loved the books which he had collected and the college to which he bequeathed them. He labored not for himself only, but for all those who seek learning. This memorial has been placed by his classmates
—Plaque placed in the Widener Memorial Library by the Class of 1907

CHAPTER 1
ALEXEI'S FINAL JOURNEY

September 20, 2012
London, England/Washington, DC

Alexei sat by the plane window and caught the day's sun. As he gazed across the vast horizon, he contemplated the events of his time in Europe and the lengthy two-year search. His mind wandered from place to place. He watched a couple of movies but became anxious and restless. He switched to the map channel on the audiovisual system. The flight simulator located the position of the plane over the city of Halifax, Nova Scotia—the city where it all began. The flight time that remained before landing at Washington's Dulles Airport was two hours and twenty-three minutes.

The interminable number 223, which had taken over his life, combined with the plane's position over Halifax, seemed to be ominous. It prompted him to reach inside his jacket and pull out the black-and-white photograph he had kept in his wallet since his visit to Harvard University in July 2011. He pondered and suddenly felt a former connection to the photograph of HEW. He stared at it resolutely. The deep-set eyes drew in Alexei as he studied the balanced facial features, the unblemished skin, the slender lips absent of a smile, the hair pulled back and smoothed down on either side of a central parting. Alexei thought that this was an impeccable model of an Edwardian gentleman.

Suddenly his thoughts were interrupted by the female passenger who was sitting next to him. "Excuse me," she said.

Alexei turned his head in surprise and saw that his previously unnoticed traveling companion was a rather large, well-dressed lady with a friendly, cheerful smile and a Southern accent.

"Excuse me. Sorry if I appear to be rude, but I couldn't help noticing the black-and-white photograph that you have been scrutinizing all this time. It looks very much like a photo I have of my great-grandfather with that dress shirt with the rounded Eton collar, the diagonally striped tie, and the jacket with large lapels. Photos from the last century always intrigue me. Is he a relative of yours?"

"No, not exactly a relative of mine." Alexei hesitated and then continued, "But we are somewhat closely connected. And yes, you are correct; he is from the last century. He was a member of a prominent Philadelphia family, the Wideners."

"Sorry, but I don't understand. If he is not a relative, then how are you connected?"

Alexei paused for a few moments. "Well," he said. He took a deep breath and sighed. "Well, that's a long, long story."

CHAPTER 2
CONCEPTION OF THE OBSESSION

July 15, 2011
Fairview Lawn Cemetery
Halifax, Nova Scotia

Alexander Julius Dante, known as Alexei to his friends and family, was sixty-five years of age and lived with his wife, Annice, in Washington, DC. Alexei looked much younger than his years. He was well-built and rather distinguished looking, with his salt-and-pepper hair and piercing, dark brown eyes. His lips curled enigmatically whenever he took on a rare smile. For nearly twenty-five of his years, he had been an associate professor at a local university.

As a retired historian, Alexei had spent several years researching tragic, historical events and, as an author, turned them into mystery novels on subjects such as Herculaneum and Pompeii and the great San Francisco Earthquake of 1906.

From a very early age he had been captivated by the *Titanic* and the events surrounding her, from her conception in London and her materialization in Belfast to her demise off the coast of Newfoundland and the final resting-place of the victims in Fairview Lawn Cemetery, Halifax. His mother first sparked his interest in the

Titanic by telling him stories about Molly Brown, the Astor family, and other well-known Americans who were on board.

He had never forgotten the movie *A Night to Remember* that he had seen when he was thirteen years of age. It had been made in 1958 and was based on the book by Walter Lord. Alexei still regarded it as one of the most historically accurate *Titanic* disaster movies.

Alexei was suffering from what one might call writer's block from his novel in progress and was in need of a break from Washington. So when the opportunity had arisen for them to take a cruise to New England and Halifax, it had seemed to be the ideal scenario to spend time together away from any distractions. At the same time, the story of what happened after the sinking would be a concluding connection to the *Titanic.*

Alexei felt excited at the thought of embarking on his own personal tour into history. At the same time, from what he had read and heard about tragedy, he had a sense of foreboding that he would be entering a mysterious and gloomy part of *Titanic*'s past. However, he was unaware that the seed of an obsession would be planted when he took a tour of Fairview Lawn Cemetery: a *Titanic* mystery that had remained unsolved for a hundred years.

The tour bus pulled up the tree-lined driveway to the entrance to the cemetery. Everyone disembarked silently. Children, teenagers, and adults made their ways respectfully to the known and unknown graves of the people whose bodies had been collected from the North Atlantic following the sinking of the *Titanic.* Although the day was gray and overcast, Alexei felt that peace and tranquility prevailed as he entered the manicured grounds. It was beautiful but somber.

He had read in all the guidebooks that there would be a large sign to indicate the victims' graves, but this had been removed and there was just a simple sign:

CITY OF HALIFAX
Fairview
Lawn
CEMETERY
1893

The tour guide indicated the sites. It was clear that this was a unique cemetery, insofar as the rows of victims were laid out in a pattern resembling the perimeter of the bow of the *Titanic*, with a vertical memorial stone at the helm. Even an opening in the formation on the right-hand side was designed to convey the point where the ship struck the iceberg. The tour guide gave a factual yet dramatic presentation, personalizing each slab of cold stone he selected.

For example, the crew of the *Mackay-Bennett,* a cable ship based in Halifax, usually repaired the underwater telegraph cables connecting North America and Europe. Suddenly they found themselves on a tragic mission: to search for and recover bodies of the victims. The ship had been contracted by the White Star Line on the evening of April 16, 1912, at a rate of $550 per day. When they came across the body of a two-year-old boy, they were so moved that they personally arranged for a stone for the child. The inscription read, "Erected to the memory of an unknown child whose remains were recovered after the disaster to the *Titanic* April 15th, 1912."

This was the beginning of an emotional experience for Alexei and Annice and the realization that this was no movie set, but reality. Tour groups had left all kinds of toys, teddy bears, and other stuffed animals around the child's grave. Although the child had been identified in 2011 through the wonders of DNA, his grave marker remained "unknown" to represent all the little children who perished with the *Titanic*. Alexei thought that surely this was one grave that would bring home the depth of the disaster to many people.

A total of 150 victims were laid to rest in the "City of Sorrow." One hundred and twenty-one victims were buried in the Protestant Fairview Lawn Cemetery, and the remaining twenty-nine victims buried in Halifax were interred in Mount Olivet Catholic Cemetery or Baron de Hirsch Jewish Cemetery.

As Alexei and Annice walked through the cemetery, they noticed many graves with newly made, white inscriptions. The graves had been subjected to detailed research over the years. As a result, a second unveiling had been held for some graves in 1991, finally giving those victims a name. A new chapter in the Halifax story could be written. However, it would take a lifetime to document all the victims. More information had to be discovered. Unfortunately for many, there would not be new information to discover.

The row upon row of victims in graves marked "unknown," not in chronological order, exacerbated the haunting adversity before their eyes. It was only then that the full extent of the tragedy hit them and gave validity to the horrific event. It was such a moving experience that Alexei knew that from then on, it would be difficult to describe in words what he truly felt.

The tour guide informed the group that there were two lists compiled shortly after the disaster and still in existence. One contained information about the 306 victims retrieved by the cable ship the *Mackay-Bennett* during its two-week search for bodies drifting around *Titanic*'s last known position. The other list had information on the identified victims on-site in Halifax or who had been shipped further.

Alexei and Annice continued with the tour group along the rows of victims, like a procession of mourners. They stopped at the first grave site, numbered 313. This was Luigi Gatti. He had been thirty-seven years old and ran two Ritz restaurants in London, the Gatti Adelphi and Gatti's Strand. His first shipboard employment had been on the *Olympic,* the sister ship to the *Titanic.* He had signed on to the *Titanic* as chef on April 6, 1912. No fewer than thirty-five Italians had been employed by Luigi Gatti on the *Titanic* as attendants, barbers, waiters, and cooks.

Suddenly Alexei stopped and stared at the small, gray, granite markers that contained just a name and date of death. What surprised him was the grave of Ernest Edward Samuel Freeman, who was listed as *Titanic*'s chief deck steward. He had actually been the personal secretary to White Star's chairman, Mr. J. Bruce Ismay, and it was he who erected the stone "to commemorate a long and faithful service."

Most of the grave markers were small. A rectangular piece of stone served as a base for each of them, with a trapezoid-shaped piece set on the base. They passed a Celtic cross, the tallest memorial among those in the *Titanic* section, which had been erected at the grave of Arthur Gordon McCrae.

Alexei and Annice moved on to another grave, numbered 227 with the name J. Dawson. It had flowers and messages from visitors who mistakenly thought that this J. Dawson was the person who had been played by Leonardo DiCaprio in James Cameron's movie, *Titanic*! In fact it belonged to twenty-three-year-old James Joseph Dawson, a trimmer on the *Titanic*'s crew who wheeled the coal for the boilers, ensuring that the fuel supplies were equally distributed so the ship would be balanced. He had joined the crew a few weeks earlier, hoping for a better life after his family was torn apart by his love for a woman they shunned. He was a Catholic, she was a Protestant, and at the turn of the century it was enough to make their love forbidden.

Alexei and Annice were now walking the same path that the American socialite Margaret Brown, known by the sobriquet "the unsinkable Molly Brown," had taken when she laid wreaths on each headstone in 1914. Alexei did not lay any wreaths. He merely put his hand on each grave as if to say, "You are not forgotten." Just as the sea had claimed its victims irrespective of class or position, so now they were buried side by side.

All the bodies recovered were numbered, and these numbers appeared on the victims' headstones. If there was no name on the headstone, then the victim had never been identified. Alexei looked at the pamphlet he had been given by the tour guide, which listed the graves. He could not understand why the graves were not in numerical order. As he read, he found out that the numbers had been given to each victim in the order in which they were brought aboard the *Mackay-Bennett*. But after leaving the Mayflower Curling Rink, the bodies became separated. Some bodies were taken to different cemeteries, some bodies were claimed, and some went directly to the undertaker's in Halifax. Others had already been buried at sea.

It was at that moment he came across a grave with the inscription:

DIED
APRIL 15, 1912
223

The number 223. The number that was of such a great significance to him. Whenever he saw it, he was drawn to it, whether on a license plate, a flight number, or a time. Why was he drawn? Who was 223?

CHAPTER 3

THE ACCIDENT

September 3, 2008
Naples, Italy/Washington, DC

Alexei recalled that his fixation with the number 223 began in September 2008 when he and Annice took a vacation to Naples, Italy. They had been experiencing serious difficulties in their marriage. There had been many infidelities, indiscretions, and selfish acts on both sides over the years. They thought they might be able to salvage something from the relationship in their twilight years by spending some quality time together. Things were going well as they hiked along the dusty, graveled road to the summit of Mount Vesuvius. Contrary to popular belief, it was neither the highest nor the most dangerous volcano in the world, but the eruption that buried Pompeii and Herculaneum in AD 79 made it famous. As Goethe wrote of Vesuvius, "Many a calamity has happened in the world but never one that has caused so much entertainment to posterity as this one."

It was a bright, clear day, and the walk along the crumbling paths by the rickety fences afforded spectacular views of the gray-and-black lava stone in the crater and of the Bay of Naples and the city.

The following day they toured the Blue Grotto in Capri, where the refraction of sunlight gave a blue iridescence to the water. They decided to take the funicular from Marina Grande to the village of Capri for a leisurely lunch at one of the flower-decked terraces overlooking the rugged cliffs along the coast.

After lunch, rather than taking the bus via numerous hairpin bends, they decided to take the chairlift to Anacapri, the island's other main village. They had been informed that this was a good spot for views over the whole island.

It was then that disaster struck. Shortly after they began the ascent, there was a loud grating noise and the chairlift unexpectedly shuddered, swung precariously over the trees, and finally came to an abrupt halt. Alexei looked up and saw that one of the main cable lines had frayed. Annice screamed and grabbed Alexei's arm. They both clung to the central pole between them. The cable finally snapped, and they fell fifty feet to the terrain below like they were in a plunging elevator. Their surroundings became blurred and distorted as they went into shock.

Alexei picked himself up and helped Annice to her feet. Both felt nauseous and dizzy but only received cuts, scratches, and multiple bruises. It was fortuitous that the ground on which they had landed was soft turf. For a few moments they wandered around like the living dead. Their senses seemed to have shut down, and they became totally disoriented. Then came a deafening silence.

After a while, Alexei was aware of people crowding around them, but he heard their voices at a distance, like one hears when first coming out of an anesthetic.

Paramedics were soon on the scene and took them to the local hospital. Following a thorough checkup and X-rays by the doctor, they were both discharged and advised to go back to their hotel and rest. It was at that moment that they both realized they could have been taken away from one another in an instant.

Annice continued to have headaches and dizziness during the following days, so they decided to catch an early flight home to Washington. After landing at Dulles Airport, they made their way to the baggage area. Annice complained of a severe headache, so Alexei suggested that she sit on the seat just behind him while he went to the carousel for their baggage. When he had put their cases onto a cart, he turned around. Annice had disappeared. He looked through the maze of people. At first he thought she might have gone to the restroom. Suddenly he heard people shouting.

"Call 911," someone yelled.

"Does anyone know this woman?" shouted another.

"She's out cold. Give her some space. Is there anyone who can help?"

Alexei casually walked over to the crowd to see what was going on and found to his horror that it was Annice. She had collapsed and was unconscious.

"Oh my God! Annice. Oh my God!" he cried. "That's my wife. Will someone please help?" he shouted, trembling with fear.

Alexei held her hand and tried to comfort her. She was lying motionless and almost lifeless. Her pupils were dilated; her eyes just stared into oblivion. Her face was slightly distorted and ashen, and she was cold to the touch. He could not get any response from her.

Alexei was beginning to panic when a quiet voice behind him said, "Excuse me, sir. I'm a medical student. Can I help? Please don't lift her. Help me to just turn her gently on her side into the recovery position. That way, she won't choke, and her airways will be kept clear. The ambulance is already on its way. What's your wife's name?"

"A-Annice," he stuttered.

"Annice! Annice, can you hear me?" asked the student. He put his head close to her to see if she was breathing.

"She's breathing, but her pulse is very weak," he reassured Alexei.

The ambulance arrived within a short time. One of the senior medics assessed her condition and fixed an oxygen mask on her before transferring her into the ambulance.

"Does she have a history of diabetes?" asked the medic, wondering whether she had an insulin deficit.

"No, nothing like that," Alexei replied.

"Do you know of any reason how or why this could have happened? Has she had any injury to her head recently?"

"Well, we were involved in a chairlift accident in Italy last week. We were seen by the doctors there and discharged from the hospital within hours with only minor injuries. However, now that I come to think about it, Annice has been complaining about dizziness and severe headaches for a few days. That's why we decided to come home. She has also been vomiting."

"It's all right, sir. Just fasten the seat belt, stay seated, and try to relax. Annice is now in good hands, and we'll be at St. Rose of Lima's Hospital in a few minutes."

Alexei's heart was racing as he sat with her in the back of the ambulance while the medical team attended to her. After a few hours, she still hadn't regained consciousness and was transferred to intensive care.

The intensive care unit at St. Rose's had been newly refurbished. The ten-bed facility offered state-of-the-art management for critically ill patients and postoperative, high-dependency care, including the latest model of ventilators, of which Annice was in need. There was an area for relatives. Smart glass allowed for observation of the patient but ensured that privacy was maintained when required.

Even though the doctor had reassured Alexei that the ICU was led by a group of dedicated and experienced critical care consultants who would provide twenty-four-hour cover for Annice by a team of specialist nurses, he could not accept the situation. He was in shock, frightened, and apprehensive. It had made him realize how tenuous life was. He felt anger, denial, and guilt. He sat down and relived the day's events and how they could have been different, in a futile attempt to change them.

As the sun arose, the doctor persuaded Alexei to go and get some rest, as nothing more could be done at the time. It was just a question of wait and see.

On his return home, he was in a state of disbelief. He wondered how quickly it had all came about. He closed the door to his apartment with his back and dropped their suitcases in the hall. The apartment seemed cold and empty. He could not bear to unpack, as the day's stress had caused him to feel extremely fatigued. Even the thought of entering the bedroom only compounded his misery.

He settled down on Annice's side of the bed and breathed in her scent. Flashbacks of the ambulance, the journey to the hospital, and the sight of Annice lying there on the clinical white sheets and connected to various machines filled his thoughts. He wondered whether the doctors should be doing more for her.

Finally, overcome by nervous exhaustion, he succumbed to a restless sleep and dreamed of Annice and their time together. She appeared to him and told him that she would only be away from him for a short time. He even felt her warm touch as she spoke. To Alexei she was real. She was there with him for the moment. He awoke to realization of the actuality of it all. How could he go on? Life without Annice was inconceivable. All those years gone in a moment.

He sat up and looked at the photograph on the dresser of the two of them, taken a few weeks after they had first met at the university in

1986. Annice had been invited to the modern languages department to promote the diplomatic corps and recruit more linguists. It was lunchtime and the student union was crowded. Alexei was carrying his tray across the room, anxiously looking for a table, when he saw an attractive woman sitting on her own with an empty seat opposite her.

"Is this seat taken?" he asked tentatively. "There don't seem to be any spare places today."

She lifted her head, flicked her long blonde hair from her face, and looked at him with her piercing blue eyes.

"No. It's free. Please, do sit down," she replied.

After about half an hour's conversation, they found that they shared artistic commonalities. Also there was a mutual physical attraction.

Both were pressed for time. The short encounter was such a gratifying experience that they exchanged business cards.

That was the beginning of a three-year courtship that culminated in marriage in 1989. They had continued to follow their careers, which involved a long-distance relationship from time to time as Annice's work frequently took her abroad.

Alexei's thoughts returned to the present. He looked at the collage on the wall: photos of their life together. He noticed that the smiles seemed to have diminished with time. Was this a sign of the demise of the relationship that he hadn't noticed before?

He pondered as to whether fate or they themselves would conclude the relationship.

For the first couple of weeks, Alexei visited Annice every day. There was no change. She remained in a coma and connected to machines. They emitted a variety of sounds, such as bleeps and alarms that concerned him.

He had been assured that the sounds just alerted the nurses when something needed attention. Because of Annice's head injury, the pressure inside her head needed to be monitored, and that accounted for the frequent bleeps.

Alexei had so many unanswered questions. Would she wake up? Would she remember what happened? When would he know how bad the head injury was? All the doctor said was "Wait and see," which seemed cruel and uncaring but was the accurate answer.

When Alexei was not at the hospital, he tried to occupy himself with routine chores, responding to correspondence from well-wishers and forcing himself to go to the store. Nothing seemed to ease his pain. He was going through emotional hell. Even his writing had become mundane. Life's priorities seemed to have changed. It was a metamorphosis of pain into grief and then to death.

***

Alexei isolated himself from his family and friends and either ignored their phone calls or brushed them off. Finally, weeks later, Alexei's close friend Ernesto became so concerned that he decided to visit him.

When Alexei opened the door, Ernesto could not believe his eyes. Alexei was in a serious physical and emotional state and was obviously not coping with the situation at all. He was unshaven, his clothes were soiled, and his hair was disheveled and in need of a trim. More significant to Ernesto was that the usually pristine apartment was in total chaos. Alexei appeared as a ghost of a figure—gaunt and thin with an ashen complexion.

Ernesto quickly surmised that Alexei was in need of help before it was too late. He felt that he must intervene. He had seen Alexei in the depths of depression a few times in the past, but nothing could compare with his present state of mind. He feared that he might have suicidal thoughts.

Ernesto suggested that they spend the day together and take in an exhibit at the National Gallery as a diversion. He was surprised when Alexei agreed.

It was a bright, cold, and brisk February day. The air was clean and fresh to inhale.

Alexei said little at the gallery. Usually he was drawn to the works of art as though he were being transported into their subject matter, but on this occasion there was no release from his pain. He was in the final stages of mourning, as he was convinced that Annice was dying. It was all over. Her requiem had begun for him.

He recalled the lines of an anonymous poet whose writings had inspired him in the past and now summed up his present feelings, for which he had no words of his own at the time.

Into a deep, quiet sleep,
Motionless and still,
Time within hours,
Years without seasons,
Breathless, inept, subdued.
A world without life,
Humanity without hope,
A trinity of the nine muses frozen.
Music without sound,
Painting without hue,
Literature without words.
Without the covenant of love all is dead.

Suddenly his thoughts were interrupted by the vibration of his cell phone.

CHAPTER 4

THE DECISION

February 23, 2009
Washington, DC

The call was from Maggie Mullins, who was Annice's assigned nurse, advising him that the doctor wanted to speak with him as soon as possible. It was the call that he had dreaded for so long. Every time his phone had rung, he had answered it with trepidation. Would this be the beginning of his torment and anguish? Would it be an answer to his prayer for Annice? Had she come through, or would he have to let go? Over the past few weeks, he had constantly told her that it was okay to let go.

Alexei had prepared well for this day, just as he had always done when faced with the death of a loved one or, as in his younger days, with the termination of a relationship.

With his heart beating rapidly and his whole body shaking, he gave Ernesto an inarticulate explanation for his impending departure, fled the gallery, and took a cab to the hospital, wondering what he was going to find on his arrival. Was she already dead? He had been given no information over the phone.

Suddenly the tears began to flow. Reality set in. His best friend, his soul mate, the person he really loved and needed, might no longer be there to support him. A void filled him. The arguments, irritations, and infidelities were dismissed as totally irrelevant to their relationship.

On arrival at the hospital, Alexei was shown into Dr. Joseph's office, where he had been summoned to discuss the possibility of turning off the life-support machine. He faced an agonizing decision, the most difficult and heart-wrenching decision he had ever had to make. It was too much for him to bear. Life without her would be unimaginable.

Dr. Joseph informed him that some patients never regained consciousness. Others recovered and had permanent brain damage. On the other hand, some patients came out of comas they had been in for weeks and, after a rehabilitation program, made a full recovery.

It was a time of real suffering for Alexei. Would this be passive euthanasia? Many questions went through his mind.

By keeping Annice on life support, would he be helping her to live longer at the expense of her comfort and dignity? What if a miracle occurred while she was on life support and she recovered? Alexei had heard of many such miracles.

He had to evaluate his own goals. He had never discussed life-sustaining treatments with her. What would she want? It was even more problematical for him to make an informed decision, as Annice had never given him a directive. It was never considered.

The other problem was that Annice had no living relatives with whom he could discuss the situation. He was alone.

Dr. Joseph suggested that he talk to a social worker or a hospital chaplain to help him face this horrendous situation. The doctor had already recommended that he get some emotional support. He even gave Alexei a list of support groups for people who had already gone through the same experience.

Alexei knew that he could only make the decision he felt was best for both of them at the time. Did he have enough love to let her go? She was existing, not living.

His Catholic upbringing kicked in, which favored no removal of life-support systems. He was even more determined to be there, tell her how much he loved her, and say good-bye. Deep down, he knew that it was not about what the living wanted, but what the dying decided that mattered. The one consolation to him was that he instinctively felt that she was in no pain. He had spent hours just looking at her over the months, and it seemed to him that she was in a suspended state of tranquility in a timeless place.

Alexei entered the room where his Annice lay. He was greeted with that everyday sound of the heart monitor—the only indication of her living being. She looked serene in spite of all the tubes and equipment to sustain her fragile life. He took the yellow roses that he had brought with him and discarded the old ones, walked over to the window, and opened the blinds to let in the early-morning light—a ritual he had done for many months.

He pulled a chair close to her bed. He gently took her hand in a prayerlike position within his hands and spoke to her softly, as he had done almost every day.

"Annice, please help me to make this decision. What am I to do?" He began to sob profusely. Suddenly he felt a twitch from her fingers. Was it his imagination, or was she responding somehow? He had been told that people in a coma were sometimes able to hear and understand. He turned his head and gazed at her. Then unexpectedly she opened her eyes, which appeared to smile at him.

"Oh my God! Annice! Thank you, God!"

In a state of shock and disbelief, he rushed out of the room and ecstatically called the duty nurse. His heart pounded with exhilaration and he could not contain his excitement, joy, and relief. He realized how much he had nearly lost. He was determined to do everything possible to support her rehabilitation and, more importantly, to sustain a relationship that meant more than he had ever known.

The day was February 23, or 2/23. So it was understandable why 223 was such a significant number and had such an important influence on Alexei's life.

Dr. Joseph called Alexei into his office and talked him through the stages of recovery for Annice. Coming out of a coma was not just waking up, as people sometimes imagined. It was a gradual process of regaining contact with the world.

He suggested that once Annice had been discharged, she should attend a rehabilitation center, where several hours a day would be devoted to specific therapy. Problems with complex thinking, emotional instability, and personality changes were common among coma patients, so Alexei would have to be patient and understanding. Recovery from a head injury such as Annice's would continue for several months, and there was the possibility of long-term problems when she went home.

Alexei listened to what the doctor was saying but didn't really hear it. His thoughts were on Annice and that she had opened her eyes.

"Alexei! Alexei!" the doctor called, trying to regain his attention. "It is important that you understand what I am saying. Changes are going to take place gradually. Yes, her eyes have opened, which is a positive sign, but she still does not have the ability to speak or follow commands. It is imperative that you remain patient and understand the situation. One of the most striking things about recovery of consciousness is that it can take some time to begin to restore the memory."

"Will she know me? Will she remember anything?" Alexei asked tentatively.

"Again, it is too soon to say. She may not remember what occurred just a few minutes or hours before the accident. There are no answers at present."

"Thanks for your time, Doctor. I apologize for asking so many questions, but I've been to hell and back over the last few months and now I can see signs of hope. Today I feel that I have been reborn. I can see the light of tomorrow."

The following day, Alexei returned to the hospital. He rushed along the maze of cold, stone-walled corridors to the ward, feeling nervous and apprehensive. To his surprise, most of the tubes had been removed. Annice was breathing by herself with just the aid of a nasal cannula. Its two thin plastic tubes were placed in her nostrils, giving her oxygen.

Alexei settled down in the chair and just watched her as she slept. That was all he could do at present. Nurse Mullins came in the room to check on the monitors.

"Can I get you some coffee or tea? A soft drink?" she asked.

"Yes, thank you," he replied. "I'll take a black coffee. Isn't this wonderful to see? I know it's early days, but now there is hope."

"To be sure there is, thanks be to God," she replied in her broad Irish accent.

Maggie had been a great source of strength to Alexei during the months that Annice had been in her care. They had developed a trusting relationship.

***

Two weeks had elapsed since February 23, when Annice had first opened her eyes. Alexei continued to visit every day, hoping that there would be some progress. Perhaps she would recognize him and ultimately respond to his voice.

He picked up his newspaper, and looked through the Home section of the *Washington Post*, and drank his coffee.

"Alexei. Alexei," came a feeble, repressed, and wavering voice.

Alexei jumped up. She had spoken his name. It was Annice's first word after all those weeks.

"Annice! I am here," he called, hardly able to restrain himself. He leaned over the bed, took her hand, stroked her hair, and kissed her forehead. "Oh, my darling I am here. I love you." He sighed, "Thank God."

CHAPTER 5

THE QUEST BEGINS

July 11, 2011
Halifax, Nova Scotia

So it was understandable why, out of the 121 grave sites, Alexei was naturally drawn to this one—number 223.

Another extraordinary coincidence, which he hadn't realized until the tour guide pointed it out, was that there were two thousand, two hundred, and twenty-three passengers and crew on board the Titanic when she sank—2223.

Alexei touched the headstone of 223. As his fingertips glided along the inscription, he wondered, "Who are you? Why am I beginning to feel a special connection with you? Why do I experience such an inexplicable feeling when I touch your grave?"

It was here that he sensed that he had to unravel a mystery. Again, he thought, *Who are you?* He felt compelled to discover the identity of the person in grave 223. The leaflet, "Titanic Cemeteries in Halifax," identified 223 only as a "crew member." In 1912 the doctor on the *Mackay-Bennett* described him as "approximately twenty-seven-year-old male with no physical identification."

As they continued their visit, Alexei was once again overtaken by melancholy. Half the people buried there still remained unidentified.

This was the second time his disbelief had been validated by fate. It made him feel an affinity for the victims. He had often heard survivors of tragic events say, "I can't believe this has happened." It was hard for anyone to accept a horrific tragedy as a reality. For him, September 11 had validated the incredulity of the *Titanic* disaster. It was only when he experienced that horrific event that the unbelievable became believable, and he could fully comprehend why they found the sinking of the *Titanic* inconceivable. Even now he still could not believe September 11 had really happened. But, having experienced the events of September 11, he was able to accept the tragedy.

His thoughts went out to the people of Halifax who had attended the burials, which started on Friday, May 3, 1912. They had wanted to offer sympathy to the unfortunate souls buried so far from their homes and their families.

As Alexei and Annice left the Fairview Lawn Cemetery, a group of schoolchildren arrived. It was of some consolation to Alexei that the memories would be continued.

They returned to the *Caribbean Princess* to continue their cruise to Boston with troublesome thoughts about the day's experience in Fairview Lawn Cemetery. Alexei needed some air. He excused himself from the dining table and went out on deck. As he leaned over the deck rail, looking at the ocean, he felt Annice's reassuring hand on his shoulder.

"Are you okay?" she asked. "You were so quiet at dinner that even our dining companions remarked on it after you left."

"Yes, I'm fine," he replied. Annice was not convinced.

"Something seems to be wrong. Do you want to talk about it?"

"When we were at the cemetery and stopped at grave 223, it brought back the memory of the day you came out of your coma. I just thought how fortunate we are that fate gave us a second chance."

"Yes, we are," she said, hugging him. "The victims and their families were not so lucky."

The words of the service for burial at sea kept reverberating in his mind: "The Sea shall give up her dead and the corruptible bodies of those who sleep shall be changed."

Their visit to Halifax was over. The fatal maiden voyage of the *Titanic* and the loss of 1,522 lives were well-known and documented. What was unknown to them both was the role that Halifax would continue to play in unraveling the identity of grave 223.

That was how and where Alexander J. Dante's obsession began—an obsession that would have an overpowering influence over his life and his relationship with Annice.

CHAPTER 6

INTRODUCTION TO HEW

July 13, 2011
Cambridge, Massachusetts

Their next port of call was Boston. It was on another guided tour, this time of Cambridge, Massachusetts, and Harvard University, that they found themselves outside the Harry Elkins Widener Memorial Library. This impressive Beaux Arts brick building, designed by one of Alexei's favorite eminent architects, Horace Trumbauer and Associates from Philadelphia, was located on the south side of the Harvard Yard, opposite the Memorial Church. Trumbauer had designed several houses for the intertwined Elkins and Widener families of Philadelphia and for other elites families. The library was the centerpiece of the Harvard University library system—the largest private academic library system in the world, with fifty-seven miles of bookshelves and three million volumes.

The library was dedicated on June 2, 1915, and opened on June 24. It had been built in memory of Harry Elkins Widener, a bibliophile who perished in the *Titanic* disaster. Harry had graduated from Harvard in 1907. Upon his death, he had bequeathed his collection of books to Harvard University with the proviso that the university could store them.

Harry's last will and testament, written on October 6, 1909, stated:

> I give and bequeath to my mother, absolutely, all my property of every kind and description. It is, however, my desire, as expressed to her, that whenever in her judgment Harvard University will make arrangements for properly caring for my collection of books, she shall give them to said University to be known as "the Harry Elkins Widener Collection." I appoint my father, George D. Widener, Executor of this my Will.

Alexei wondered whether Harry had had a premonition that he would predecease his parents.

Harry's mother, Eleanor Elkins Widener, had donated over $3 million to the construction, with the stipulation that the library could never be changed once built: "Not a brick, stone, or piece of mortar shall be changed." The library was a mother's tribute to her son and the fulfillment of his strongest wish.

Although Eleanor Elkins Widener accomplished her two objectives, completing her son's library and seeing it rightly housed at Harvard, her sense of loss was never completely alleviated. Years later she wrote to Flora Livingston, wife of Luther Livingston, who became the librarian of the library after the death of her husband in 1914, "I cannot stay long away from the library—I feel nearer to my boy when I am there."

Their tour guide had irritated them both, giving out so much incorrect historical and geographical information that they decided to leave the tour and make their own way back to the ship.

They had a few hours to spare, and, as they were right outside the library, Annice suggested, "You have always wanted to visit the library. Now you have the opportunity. Go for it! After all, it is another *Titanic* connection."

They climbed the steps to the entrance and arrived at the reception desk. However, the strict conditions for entry to the library were that one had to be either a published author or a bona fide research student from the world of academia. Because of these constraints Annice was unable to join him and had to remain outside. Alexei hesitated; disappointed that Annice could not share this with him.

"Go ahead. I'll make a few calls and catch you later. Take your time," she said as she made her way down the steps.

As he looked through the central doorway, he saw a vista of marble columns. On the left-hand side of the vestibule to the main entrance of the library was the following inscription:

HARRY*ELKINS*WIDENER
A GRADUATE OF
THE UNIVERSITY
BORN JANUARY *3* 1885
DIED AT SEA APRIL *15* 1912
UPON THE FOUNDERING
OF THE STEAMSHIP
TITANIC

On the right hand side of the vestibule, the inscription read:

THIS LIBRARY
ERECTED
IN LOVING MEMORY OF
HARRY * ELKINS * WIDENER
BY HIS MOTHER
ELEANOR ELKINS WIDENER

DEDICATED
JUNE *24* 1915

Another memorial read, "Harry Elkins Widener, AD 1907, loved the books which he had collected and the college to which he bequeathed them. He labored not for himself only, but for all those who seek learning. This memorial has been placed by his classmates."

Alexei walked up the marble steps to the Widener Memorial Rooms. As he entered the rotunda, which was in the center of the building on the mezzanine between the first and second floors, two fourteen-foot-high murals occupying two arched panels on either side of the door caught his eye. *Death and Victory* and *The Coming of the Americans to Europe* had been commissioned by Harvard as part of the university's tribute to the World War One dead and painted by John Singer Sargent. Alexei had always admired Sargent's bright, insightful portraits of society debutantes and his watercolors that captured the beauty of American and European landscapes, but had not seen his famed murals.

There was an inscription over the door to the rotunda that led into the HEW Memorial Room:

TO THE MEMORY OF
ELEANOR ELKINS RICE
WHOSE NOBLE AND ENDEARING SPIRIT
INSPIRED THE CONCEPTION AND COMPLETION
OF THIS MEMORIAL LIBRARY
1938

He walked into a circular area, the outer of the two rooms, made of Alabama marble with the exception of the domed ceiling. There were four glass display tables arranged around the room in recesses that could have contained statuaries. The first display table contained memorabilia of Harry's birth, his time at Harvard, and the undergraduate theatrical society, the Hasty Pudding Club. Researching costumes had sparked Harry's interest in extra-illustrated and costume books. The culmination of Harry's acting career had been his role as Mr. Abadiah Burdock Butterworth in a production of *The Lotus Eaters* in 1907. The script and music had been written by club members.

The second case contained Harry's book purchase ledger and his first serious purchase: a presentation copy of the third edition of Charles Dickens's *Oliver Twist*. There was a copy of a letter from Harry to his friend Luther Livingston, the New York bookseller, dated March 10, 1912, telling him that Harry was about to take "a trip to England on the *Mauretania,* returning on the maiden voyage of the *Titanic* on April 10." He was making the journey to purchase a rare second-edition copy of Francis Bacon's *Essaies* of 1598.

Near the end of the letter, he told Livingston "a secret, grandfather has bought the Hoe copy on paper of the Mazarin Bible. Is it not great? I wish it were for me but it is not." Alexei felt a sense of sadness knowing that this "Hoe copy" of the book, better known as the Gutenberg Bible, had finally come into the Widener Collection.

The third table displayed information on the sinking and memorials of the *Titanic.* Alexei had read gripping accounts of the disaster over the years, but what had always intrigued him was what happened to the survivors and how the cataclysmic event affected their lives. The wreck of the *Titanic* always overshadowed the lives of the 705 survivors. Little was ever mentioned of the fact that the tragedy signaled the end of an era of immense wealth, opulence, and privilege. The mighty ship was the swan song of an era soon to be blown apart by World War One.

The fourth case was devoted to the intricate details of the building of the library.

Alexei was stopped at the entrance to the library by a balustrade on an imperial-looking, red Persian Heriz rug. He absorbed his surroundings. He found the special English oak panels, carved in their native land and then brought over panel by panel, particularly interesting. The high bookcases were fitted with glass shelves and bronze sashes; the windows were hung with heavy curtains; and the shelves held three thousand volumes of rare books, mainly by nineteenth-century English authors, including extra-illustrated books.

Beyond the balustrade, on permanent display in a glass case, was a copy of *Mr Shakespeare's Comedies, Histories and Tragedies*, better known as the Locker-Van Antwerp First Folio of Shakespeare of 1623, and also the Gutenberg Bible printed in Mainz around 1458.

The Gutenberg Bible had been the first major work printed in Europe with movable metal type, and was the most valuable book in the collection. HEW's grandfather, Peter Arrell Brown Widener, had bought the Bible when Harry was in London. He wanted to surprise Harry with it, but Harry never returned. It was donated to the library after his death. The book was open to St. Paul's Letter to the Corinthians: "and the dead shall be raised incorruptible." This sent shivers down Alexei's spine. He thought that the whole room seemed to be more like a mausoleum without a body than a library.

Above the fireplace was a haunting portrait of Harry by Gabriel Ferrier of Paris, who reproduced it from a photograph in 1913. Alexei was spellbound. Harry was perfectly groomed, his head slightly tilted and supported by his hand. He was perched forward as if he wanted to be accessible—not distant or aloof, as portraits can often appear. The piercing, deep-set eyes, which seemed to be looking into his soul, made Alexei feel uneasy. There seemed to be a yearning to communicate, coupled with a sense of loss that could not be explained. Somehow, Alexei felt that he knew Harry—but from where?

He continued to look around. On the right-hand side of the fireplace was a table with two photographs of Harry and his mother.

On the left was a desk with a vase of fresh flowers, which were replaced weekly in accordance with the wishes of the family. There was also an art nouveau, unsigned, stained-glass Tiffany lamp that reflected the light and gave some semblance of life to an otherwise murky room.

Before leaving the library, he took one final glance at the portrait. It was then that he noticed that Harry was holding a book in his left hand and resting it on his knee. He wondered, "Is that book the little Bacon that he would carry to his watery grave?" Something was telling him that this book was of significance.

Suddenly his thoughts were interrupted as he remembered his appointment with a curator at the Museum of Fine Arts in Boston. She had given a lecture on John Singer Sargent in Washington and, as Alexei had visited Sargent's grave site in Woking, England, he had taken a photograph for her. He glanced at his watch and felt a chill. It was 2:23 p.m. That number again.

The pathos that he had experienced in Fairview Lawn Cemetery suddenly resurfaced. Why? His thoughts and feelings seemed to be related to his curiosity over grave 223. He knew that he had to find out more about HEW and what had happened to him and the book. Was there any connection between the two?

Full of excitement and enthusiasm, he bounded down the steps, eager to share his thoughts and findings with Annice.

"What's the matter? What happened in there? You're so pale," she asked as she took his hand. "And you're all cold and clammy. Are you unwell?"

"No, no," he stammered. "I'm fine. I'm just so excited. I can't explain now. Let's go to the Museum of Fine Arts; otherwise we'll be late for my appointment."

Alexei had a sixth sense that there was more to this story than he had realized.

CHAPTER 7
THE RECONCILIATION

August 6, 2011
Viareggio, Italy

Alexei and Annice had made a great effort to rebuild their lives but with some considerable difficulty. He tried very hard to be patient with her and give her the benefit of the doubt, allowing that the head injury, medication, and trauma from the accident were partially responsible for her violent mood swings and unpredictability. Most of the time she was loving, giving, and caring, but there were times when her behavior frightened him, causing much pain.

For his part, he knew that he was not entirely blameless and would pick up her every mistake, however trivial, just to provoke a reaction. This was a cause of the underlying tension between them.

They decided to take a vacation to Europe. In spite of the accident and painful memories of the previous year, they both loved Italy. It was a spontaneous decision to make Tuscany their destination, with its archetypal landscapes and all its artistic history, museums, and palaces. Deep down, they knew that they had too much in common to give up on their relationship after all these years. Alexei hoped that it might be a new beginning for them. As Annice had to be in Florence for a conference, Alexei would meet her in Pisa two weeks after her arrival there. He hoped that they would benefit from some space before their vacation.

Alexei felt rather dispirited as they said good-bye at Washington's Dulles Airport, but at the same time he knew that they would be with one another again the following week. They had reserved tickets for the annual Giacomo Puccini Opera Festival, first staged in 1930, which was held in Torre Del Lago, close to Viareggio and the Tuscan countryside. Here they could share their love of opera, which expressed an emotional connection, and restore what they loved. He hoped music would regenerate the feelings they had once had and the reasons they had fallen in love. Neither of them had any inkling as to what awaited them or what would transpire.

When Annice met Alexei at the airport in Pisa, he was pleased to see her again. They chatted and laughed on the journey to their accommodation. It was like old times. Things appeared to be going well, they were both relaxed, and there was no evidence of any tension in the relationship.

Viareggio was the southernmost Riviera-style resort tucked away in Northern Tuscany on the coast of the Tyrrhenian Sea and the largest beach town in Tuscany. Sometimes called Tuscany's Biarritz, it is a serene, peaceful, and rejuvenating location with its art nouveau buildings, shops, and cafés, which they loved. They thought of the town as Florence-on-Sea, particularly because of its sedate locality, the beaches of golden sand, marinas, and vast pine woods.

"Oh look! Ice cream," Alexei cried, pointing toward a little French ice cream parlor. "How about some ice cream? They make it with egg yolks over here." He stopped the car.

"No, thank you," she replied. "And anyway, what's the difference? Can you really tell?"

"Yes, of course you can," he retorted. "Did you know it was Dolley Madison who popularized ice cream? She introduced it to

America, but without eggs in the ingredients. Are you sure you won't have some?" He took a large cone from the vendor. "Go on; have a lick. You know you want to," he persisted.

"Oh, all right," she agreed as she seductively took a lick from the side of the cone. "Mmmm—it's good!"

Alexei laughed as he wiped her mouth with his napkin. "Have another lick."

"No, thanks. I'm good," she said. She chuckled and blushed.

Alexei was very tired after his long journey, so they decided to eat in that night. Annice cooked a meal while he took a nap. It was like old times when they used to talk and joke over dinner.

They had rented the Villa Francesco, just outside Lucca, for the duration of the opera festival. It dated back to the nineteenth century and had been restored by a rich American widow at the beginning of the twentieth century. It had wonderful panoramic views of the Bagni di Lucca city center.

The furnishings had been carefully selected. They were sober and typical of the Lucca villas of the eighteenth and nineteenth centuries. Annice loved the bathroom, which was fitted with Carrera marble and ornaments of different colors.

The staircase had two landings with large bookshelves containing hundreds of books about the history of Lucca, as well as a collection of Italian and English novels dating back to the nineteenth century. Among them was a copy of Robert Louis Stevenson's *Treasure Island.* Alexei recalled that in the Harvard library, there had been a reference to the copy that HEW had obtained.

He pondered. *Books, bookshelves, private book collections—is there no escape from the association with HEW?*

The following day, they drove four miles to Torre di Lago to visit the Villa Puccini. The composer had built it in 1900, after the success of *La Bohème*, as a refuge of peace and tranquility. It was here that he lived and composed his major operas until the pollution from the lake forced him to move to Viareggio.

Puccini's granddaughter, Simonetta—a well-built lady with rosy cheeks, a welcoming smile, and a cat that was draped around her neck like a stole—greeted them and showed them around the villa. Alexei was excited as he told her of the statue of Cho-Cho San that he had seen at Glover House in Nagasaki when he served in the United States Navy. He described the statue to her and she was enthralled. The opening scene of Puccini's *Madame Butterfly* was set on a hillside overlooking the harbor and city of Nagasaki, where Lieutenant Pinkerton of the United States Navy contracted to marry a fifteen-year-old geisha girl, Cho-Cho San, known as Butterfly.

Simonetta showed them photographs that she had of Madame Butterfly's house in Nagasaki and this triggered Alexei's memory. He told her about Thomas Glover, a Scotsman who married a Japanese woman and brought the railway to Nagasaki and also the Mitsubishi Steel Works. His palatial house that visitors would have walked to in Puccini's day could now be reached by moving walkways. The gardens were dazzling, and the statue of Butterfly looked graceful dressed in her kimono. She had one protective hand on the shoulder of her son, whom she would hand over to Lieutenant Pinkerton, her faithless American husband in the opera. Her other hand was pointing toward the harbor where his ship would come in. In the corner was a cameo of Puccini.

They continued the tour of the villa. In one room there were four large showcases containing mementos, letters, photographs, documents, Puccini's ashtray, pencil, and spectacles, and original autographed scores of his musical compositions. In a corner was his favorite Forster piano, which had given birth to his heavenly melodies.

Simonetta took them into the small chapel where Puccini was laid to rest. It was transformed into a mausoleum after his death.

Antonio Puccini, his only son, had the chapel built inside the villa and placed Puccini's remains there on November 29, 1926, two years after his death. Later, Elvira, his wife, and Antonio and his wife, Rita Dell'Anna, were also buried in the chapel.

Suddenly Alexei experienced a sense of déjà vu and froze, unable to move. It was an eerie feeling. There were fresh flowers in front of Puccini's green marble tomb. Above it, and on the opposite wall, were two admirable female figures in white marble by the sculptor Maraini representing respectively Music and Opera. He remembered the two murals by Sargent in the rotunda at the HEW Memorial library and made a comparison of the two in his mind.

Above the altar in the Puccini chapel was a glass case representing the risen Christ. On the facing wall was a mosaic *Allegory of the Soul* and below it a stoup, both by Adolfo De Carolis, one of the most important Liberty artists. Alexei was captivated. The ceiling was decorated in oriental style like a "great decorated fabric of gold background." They were both struck by the preciousness and harmony of the embellishments of the room.

This was another mausoleum—another reminder—another connection to HEW. *What is this obsession with HEW that even haunts me on vacation?* he thought. Unanswered questions troubled him as they continued the tour.

Prior to attending a first-night performance of *Madame Butterfly*, they had dinner at the Château del Lago restaurant on the lake in front of the villa across from the Festival Theater. Puccini himself had visited it so frequently that it became an important part of his memoirs. It was still a meeting point for artists and musicians. The Macchiaioli frescoes added to the ambience of the restaurant. Alexei had not realized that this group of painters from Tuscany, who were active in the nineteenth century and forerunners of the impressionists, had been commemorated here.

The excellent restaurant specialized in seafood but also offered a wide selection of Mediterranean dishes. They both happily found something palatable.

After dinner they made their way to their seats for the performance. It was a true break from Alexei's obsession. The stage set against the backdrop of the Massaciuccoli Lake in front of Puccini's villa was really something to see. The flickering lights from the villages on the opposite shore and the natural scenery complemented the performance. They looked up at the starlit sky just as Pinkerton and Butterfly sang their famous duet at the end of Act One.

"*Dolce notte. Quanto stelle. Non le vidi mai si belle. Tutti estatico d'amor, ride il ciel.*" The English translation of the romantic lyrics was, "Lovely night. All those stars. I've never seen anything so beautiful. Full of the ecstasy of love, the sky smiles down."

Annice touched his hand. The duet seemed more poignant to her that night. It was if the stars themselves were gazing down on them and lighting their future. She felt that the performance was solely theirs.

Alexei did not respond. To him, the beautiful view became tainted—the flickering lights, the starlit night, and the calm water. Thoughts of that fateful night, of Harry, and of the *Titanic* filled his mind. It was an intrusion on what was to have been an experience shared with Annice.

"Where are you?" whispered Annice. "You're not here, and you're not sharing this with me, are you?"

Alexei did not answer.

"Is another vacation going to be ruined by your obsession? Answer me!"

"Please, Annice. Not now," Alexei replied as he released his hand from her touch.

"I see no difference between your obsession and an affair. I still feel that I am being shared," she added, slightly moving away from him.

Alexei made no response.

"Shh," hissed a voice from behind.

As the performance continued, the tension between them built silently. They were both uncomfortable as they returned to their villa. The evening ended with an unspoken coolness between them.

The following day was bright and sunny, but this didn't alleviate the tense atmosphere fostered during the previous evening. After breakfast they decided to visit the nearby town of Livorno to visit the Mascagnian Museo—the house of the great composer Pietro Mascagni. They both had fond memories of a performance of his opera, *Cavalleria Rusticana*, which they had heard when they were younger and their relationship was new, exciting, and optimistic—a fantasy with an unblemished future. Now there was baggage and HEW.

"Remember when we went to Ravello at dawn to hear a concert in the beautiful setting high up on the hill?" Alexei called to mind, trying to ease some of the strain that had been caused by his obsession the previous evening, which had put their relationship in retrograde again.

"Yes, I certainly do. I remember it overlooked your grandmother's village of Maiori on the Amalfi Coast," Annice recalled with a reserved smile on her face.

"I don't think we shall ever forget hearing the orchestra play the intermezzo from *Cavalleria Rusticana* just as the sun was rising. Remember in the opera that it was played when the stage was empty and all the villagers were in church?"

"Yes, and we could hear the church bell from Santa Maria a Mare—your grandmother's church—tolling in the distance."

"Again, nature's splendor provided the scenery," he mused as his mind reverted to that unprecedented morning. High up on the hill, the darkness broken by the houses in the valley below, only the voluptuous contours of the mountains could be made out. The little fishing boats added a spark of light as they returned with the night's catch.

The first hint of sunrise had been a nebulous silhouette of the mountainside, charcoal-black. As the sun began to rise, the colors became autumnal with orange, amber, and gold streaks. Then the red ball of the sun cast light into the valley so that the green hills, white stucco houses with their orange roofs, and Maiori's little church and its bells became more discernible. Dawn had begun its performance superlatively coordinated with the music of the intermezzo.

To assuage the sudden sense of melancholy that enveloped him, he suggested, pointing across the square, "Shall we take a break and have a coffee at that bar over there?"

"Good idea," she replied, taking his hand.

Annice tried to distract him by suggesting that they visit the Villa Valsorano, where the English poet Percy Bysshe Shelley stayed during the summer of 1819. She had just finished reading Mary Shelley's book *Frankenstein* and was interested to see where they had both lived.

"Did you know that because of a preface written by Percy Shelley in the first edition, many people thought that he had written *Frankenstein*, because no one could believe a nineteen-year-old woman could write such a horror story?"

"No, I didn't," replied Alexei. "I wonder what inspired her to write it?"

They walked along the Via Venuti and turned in to a narrow side street. "When did she meet Shelley then?" asked Alexei.

"Oh, she was only fifteen, and he was already married. There was some talk, you know. Ah, here it is!" exclaimed Annice, interrupting her own exegesis. "Number 23."

As they took a short tour of the museum, Alexei came across a glass case.

"Look at this!" he said to Annice. "There's a reference here to Francis Bacon's *Essaies*. You recall? HEW's treasured possession? Shelley described his writings."

"How can I forget?" she muttered as she walked into the adjacent room.

"It says, 'His language has a sweet majestic rhythm, which satisfies the sense, no less than the almost superhuman wisdom of his philosophy satisfies the intellect.'"

Alexei could not understand how these events all seemed to relate to HEW. It was almost as if he were being led from Halifax to Harvard and now to the Puccini villa, Livorno, and Shelley. But to what end? He was becoming even more obsessive about the pieces of the puzzle that were still missing. His mind was saturated with subliminal messages. He was feeling somewhat subdued and preoccupied with his thoughts as he and Annice returned to their villa before attending the second night of the Puccini Festival for a performance of *La Bohème*.

Their vacation was at an end, and after the performance Alexei and Annice relaxed over coffee and a cognac. They discussed the evening's spectacle in unresolved stress.

On the morning of their departure, they took a stroll on the promenade in Viareggio and stopped for coffee at the café that Puccini frequented when he lived there. There was a plaque on the wall outside that commemorated his visits.

There was a cool breeze from the sea and they breathed in the scent of the salted air as the seagulls squawked overhead.

As they approached the end of the promenade Alexei noticed a group of about twenty young people gathered around someone who seemed to be a tour guide. He was pointing to something near the canal that marked the boundary between Viareggio and Camaiore. As Alexei came closer, he realized that they were a group of students with their professor who were looking at a small, black cross. He paused to eavesdrop.

"Come on; let's go," Annice said, getting impatient.

"No. Wait just a minute." Alexei approached them but stopped to listen at a polite distance. It transpired that they were a group of English graduate literary students. He turned to Annice. "I want to hear this. It sounds interesting."

Annice ignored him and turned around to walk back along the promenade. Alexei listened intently to the professor, who was talking about John Milton's Cambridge friend, Edward King. King drowned in the passage of the Irish Sea and inspired the poet to write the immortal elegy "Lycidas."

The professor recited:

> Who would not sing for Lycidas? he knew
> Himself to sing, and build the lofty rhyme.
> He must not float upon his wat'ry bier
> Unwept—

Suddenly, Alexei remembered reading a copy of the newspaper headline from the London *Daily Telegraph* of June 5, 1912, which described HEW as "An 'American Lycidas': Harry Widener's Bequest to Harvard."

The professor continued as Alexei stood enraptured. "John Keats and Percy Bysshe Shelley were mutual admirers, both of the English Romantic school of poets. When Shelley heard that Keats had been taken ill with tuberculosis, he invited him to stay with his family in Pisa. Keats never reached the Shelleys as he died in Rome on February 23, 1821, at the age of twenty-five—"

Like a meteor that hits earth, Alexei was stunned. February 23—again, 2/23. This was beyond belief! The image of the gray tombstone 223 in Halifax came into his mind. Suddenly he heard the words, "At the age of twenty-nine, Shelley drowned," and immediately refocused on the professor's lecture.

"… drowned while returning from Livorno to Larici in his schooner, *Don Juan*, on July 8, 1822, during a violent thunderstorm. The boat went down quickly. Shelley thrust a copy of John Keats's poems in his jacket pocket so hard that it had doubled back at 'The Eve of St. Agnes' and the spine split. His body was cast up on the shore by the waves and was identified by his clothes, not by his face. His body was cremated on the beach at the other end of the promenade but now the land has been reclaimed from the sea. There is a monument to Shelley in Piazza Shelley. His ashes were buried in the Protestant Cemetery in Rome and on his gravestone is an appropriate quotation from Ariel's song from Shakespeare's *The Tempest*:

> Nothing of him that doth fade,
> But doth suffer a sea-change
> Into something rich and strange."

"Alexei! Alexei!" called Annice. "Come on! Let's go!"

"Just a minute," he replied curtly.

"Come on. Please! We have a plane to catch," she added demandingly.

Alexei began to make his way slowly and diffidently.

"What's the rush? We have plenty of time. I don't want to sit in the airport for hours. That was all so very interesting and relevant, and I wanted to listen."

"What was so interesting and relevant?"

"The lecturer. He was talking about Keats, who died on February 23—223 again. Yes, and another equivalence," he continued excitedly. "Shelley drowned with a copy of Keats in his pocket. HEW died with a copy of Bacon's *Essaies* in his, and I read recently that Wallace Hartley, the band leader on the *Titanic* who led the orchestra that played as the great ship went down, drowned with his most precious possession strapped to him—his violin."

An epiphany—a manifestation, a sign, an explanation, or a revelation—was taking place for Alexei, but Annice could not understand. *What does all this mean*? Alexei thought. *Where is the book? Where is the body? Where are the answers?*

Alexei put his hand on Annice's shoulder and tried to explain in a gentle tone, "Annice, I now know that I have to continue my quest to solve the mystery. Some would call it fate that is beginning to lead and guide me, but I feel that HEW is communicating in some mysterious way."

Annice's patience was now exhausted. "Enough, Alexei. Just shut the hell up! I've had it with HEW and I've had it with you," she shouted angrily. "You're not the man I married. What's happened to you? I've put up with your intolerable behavior for long enough. You've become a selfish and obsessive bastard, and unless you stop all this crazy, delusional, obsessive course of action, I want out of this marriage. Well? What do you have to say?"

"Are you threatening me? If so, you know the answer. I am not prepared to discuss anything with you while you are out of your mind. End of discussion," Alexei responded. "Now let's both calm down, go back to the villa, and pack for our flight to England."

The coolness, abruptness in conversation, and unresolved tension in the relationship continued during the flight to London.

CHAPTER 8

THE VACATION TO ENGLAND

September 6, 2011
Isle of Wight, England

The extraordinary events were once again becoming too coincidental to be just random. They seemed to be either directing Alexei or leading the way. He felt as though some powerful energy was behind this. His obsession was increasing.

During their visit to England in September of that strange summer, Alexei and Annice traveled to the Isle of Wight via Southampton. The Isle of Wight, a popular holiday destination since Victorian times, was the largest island off England, located in the English Channel just two miles from the south coast.

As the ferry left the port for Cowes, he went on deck to see Cunard's grand ocean liner, *Queen Victoria,* tied up at the very same pier where the *Titanic* and other famous liners had once been berthed. She was breathtaking to see.

Within a few hours they were on their way to visit Osborne House in East Cowes. Queen Victoria and Prince Albert had bought the Osborne estate in 1845 as a retreat to escape from court life in London and Windsor. Prince Albert's Italianate design became known as the Osborne style and was imitated throughout the British

Empire. He wanted it to be a family home by the sea and not a palace. After Albert died in 1861, Queen Victoria found solace at Osborne. When she died in 1901, it was opened up to the public.

After the visit they continued along the winding coastal road to find their accommodation.

"This is delightful," remarked Annice as they drove up the cobbled drive. "I've always wanted to stay in a typically English, cottage-style B&B." Their room was not quite ready so they left their suitcases in the lobby, which was decorated in dark mahogany with pictures of famous liners. They took afternoon tea in the lounge while they waited.

Alexei noticed that the lounge had paneling and the stairwell had heavy oak railings. The proprietor informed them that when the *Mauretania*, sister ship of the *Lusitania,* was dismantled, Metal Industries Ltd. of Glasgow purchased the ship for scrap on April 3, 1935. All the fixtures and fittings were auctioned on May 14 at Southampton Docks. The paneling used in the hotel had been salvaged from that great ship.

"Is there no getting away from these damn ships?" Annice muttered under her breath.

Alexei did not hear. His thoughts were elsewhere. A shiver ran through him. He recalled the copy of the letter from Harry Widener to his friend Luther Livingston, a New York bookseller, telling him of his trip to England to purchase books from Bernard Quaritch, the antiquarian booksellers in London. Harry had said he would sail on the *Mauretania* and return on the maiden voyage of the *Titanic.* Alexei was now able to touch the railings and panels from the first ship.

"I wonder if Harry might have also touched them," he considered as he held the railings on his way up to their room. What was this inexplicable connection that he felt between HEW and himself? His mind went back to Harry's portrait in the library at Harvard. Was Harry really trying to communicate? Everywhere Alexei turned, there was always something or some incident that seemed to be pertinent to HEW, his possible link to the unidentified grave 223 in Halifax, and Alexei's quest for more evidence.

March 1912

In March 1912, Harry and his parents left for Europe on the *Mauretania* with the valet Edwin Keeping and the maid Amalie Gieger. The crossing from New York to Liverpool was routine for Harry. The *Mauretania* had run aground on December 7, 1911, and did not resume service until March 1912.

As she left her berth and made her way up the Hudson River toward the opening of the harbor, Harry leaned against the rail, catching the cool March air. He was filled with excitement at the prospect of purchasing new books for his collection and meeting his friends, whom he had not seen since the previous summer. Meanwhile, the ship passed by historical landmarks such as Battery Park and magnificent structures, such as the Brooklyn Bridge, Ellis Island, and the Statue of Liberty.

Within half an hour, the ship was sailing on the open sea. Harry spent the ensuing five days either reading or taking long strolls on deck in spite of what he would later describe in a postcard to his friend Rosenbach as a "few rough days." He recalled the conversation he had had over lunch with Edward Newton, a self-appointed publicist, the day before he left. Norton had remarked that by the following week, Harry would be in London having lunch at the Ritz with Quaritch. Now Harry was only a train journey away from London's Euston Station and was anxious to alert his friends to his arrival.

Meanwhile, Harry's parents made their way to the London Museum to make sure that thirty silver plates, once the property of Eleanor "Nell" Gwyn, the former orange seller who had captured the heart of King Charles II of England, had been shipped safely and had arrived. The museum had been inaugurated on March 21 by King George V, Queen Mary, Princess Mary, and Prince George at Kensington Palace and was to be opened to the public on April 8.

They continued to Waterloo Station to catch the boat train to France. There they would stay at the Ritz Hotel in Paris before making their way to the Riviera. Their daughter, Eleanor, was engaged to Fitz Eugene Dixon Jr., a banker and Davis Club captain, and was due to get married in June of that year. Her wedding dress was being trimmed with special lace that had been in the family for generations. The dress itself they would purchase in France with other items for her trousseau.

Harry Widener had traveled to London specifically to keep an appointment with Bernard Quaritch, proprietor of an antiquarian bookshop that had been open since 1847 on Grafton Street in Mayfair. Quaritch had secured an exceedingly rare second-edition copy of Francis Bacon's *Essaies* of 1598 at the Huth sale. This edition was reputed to be rarer than the first edition mainly because the *Meditationes Sacrae* (Sacred Meditations) appeared in English for the first time.

While in London, Harry spent many hours with Quaritch at Sotheby's and rummaged through the dusty alcoves of numerous book shops. They also spent time in conversation and dining at the Ritz.

On March 19, a month before returning on the *Titanic*, Harry sent a postcard from the Ritz Hotel, Piccadilly, London, to his friend

Abraham Simon Wolf Rosenbach in Philadelphia. Rosenbach was a fellow bibliophile who encouraged, guided, and mentored Harry.

> Dear Doctor,
>
> Saw Mr. Quaritch this morning and found him much as he left. Still on a diet but looking a lot lighter. Also seems in much better spirits. Had a fair trip with two very rough days.
>
> Sincerely, H. E. Widener

Little did he know that the return trip would be much rougher!

Harry had begun serious book collecting during his time at Harvard University. He started with the first editions of the authors he loved, such as Charles Dickens, Robert Louis Stevenson, Percy Bysshe Shelley, and Robert Browning. He soon owned a copy of nearly everything they had written. His first serious purchase was a presentation copy of the third edition of Dickens's *Oliver Twist*. His favorite book was *Treasure Island* by Robert Louis Stevenson. Although he knew it by heart, he never traveled without it.

Later, inspired by his days as a member of the Hasty Pudding Club—a social club for Harvard students, founded in 1770, and also the nation's oldest theater company, which annually put on a spectacular spring production in drag—he became interested in Cruickshank, extra-illustrated books, costume books, and also original drawings and manuscripts.

By the age of twenty-three, he was well established in the book collecting world of the time and belonged to the Grolier Society and the Bibliophile Society. He was also in close contact with Dr. Abraham Simon Wolf Rosenbach, a rare book dealer of Philadelphia, and Luther Livingston, another book dealer from New York. He had already developed a philosophy of collecting, as he wrote to Luther Livingston on May 6, 1910: "No matter how important a book or manuscript may be I only want those that interest me."

After the death of her son, Eleanor Elkins Widener asked Luther Livingston to become the first librarian of the Harry Elkins Widener Collection in the Memorial Rooms in the center of the great library building at Harvard. The business acquaintance between bookseller and collector had begun soon after Harry graduated from Harvard. They shared a warm personal friendship. Eleanor Elkins Widener wrote, "He loved you Mr. Livingston and has talked to me so often of your knowledge and the help you were to him in advising him about books. Hundreds of times he has told me that when he could afford it, he would have you for his private librarian. You were so congenial with him and he loved working with you."

Lynnewood Hall, Elkins Park, PA

Harry Widener kept his book collection in a Louis XIV–style library in the largest room at his home at Lynnewood Hall in Elkins Park, just north of Philadelphia. His grandfather, Peter Arrell Brown Widener, had commissioned local architect Horace Trumbauer to design and build the Georgian-style, 110-room Lynnewood Hall on three hundred acres of land, for both his family and his art collection. It was completed between 1898 and 1900.

P. A. B. Widener was a great tramway magnate and became the wealthiest man in Philadelphia. He was self-taught about art but at the time of his death was worth $11 million. He owned six Van Dycks and four Rembrandts, and had paid $700,000 for the Cowper Madonna by Raphael. The house was modeled on Prior

Park in Bath, England, but it was often referred to as "the last of the American Versailles" because the decorator, William Baumgarten, spared no expense, using the family's tapestries and paintings to create a sense of Versailles. It was indeed "the house that art built," art accrued by way of Widener's accumulated wealth.

His ascent to plutocratic status from humble beginnings began when he was a butcher's boy and had saved all his money until he could buy his own shops. Then he was given a United States government contract to supply mutton to the Union troops within a ten-mile radius of Philadelphia. He took the profit and invested in horse cars with his friend William Elkins. He continued running his chain of butcher shops. Then he, William Elkins, and political boss William Kemble pooled their resources and bought street railway franchises. They founded the Philadelphia Traction Company and expanded their holdings to Chicago, Pittsburgh, and Baltimore until they operated five hundred miles of track. Widener also invested in International Mercantile Marine, owner of the White Star Line and *Titanic,* with J. P. Morgan and was organizer of the American Tobacco Company.

The library, on the first floor of the house, was finished in light oak accented with gold and surmounted by central wall panels covered in velours de Gênes. The ceiling painting, depicting angels in a cloud-swept sky, was attributed to Tiepolo and taken from an Italian palace. Above the bookshelves, paintings by Chavannes, Courbet, and Leys were displayed. After the tragedy, the library/drawing room was converted into a ballroom. Grief-stricken over the loss of his son, George Widener, and his grandson, Harry, P. A. B. Widener spent time completing Harry's book collection and planning to build a library at Harvard in his memory.

Two months after the disaster, Harry's sister Eleanor married Fitz Eugene Dixon in a simple white dress, as the trousseau bought in

France was then at the bottom of the Atlantic. They were married in the Van Dyck Gallery, the crown jewel of the home, which Widener had named after his favorite Flemish painter. It was designed to display the wealth of his family in order to give legitimacy to his status in Philadelphia society and to provide proof of his innate good taste.

A portrait of P. A. B. Widener, painted by the renowned John Singer Sargent, hung over the fireplace. When Widener died in 1915, his viewing took place in the gallery below his portrait, as instructed in his will. Three generations of the family grew up on the estate. The last, Joseph Widener, remained at the house until 1940. He made the decision to have the family's art collection displayed in the newly constructed National Gallery of Art in Washington, DC, along with diverse major contributions by other philanthropists. In that way the art could be shared by all.

Originally the paintings were hung in the Victorian fashion, frame to frame and floor to ceiling. Many of the classic masters, including Rubens, Gainsborough, and Manet, were represented. Fourteen Rembrandts were part of the collection, including *The Mill*, which he purchased for £400,000 amid controversy. The British didn't want it to leave the United Kingdom. However, as nobody could match his offer, it came to the United States of America.

The gallery adjacent to the ballroom at Lynnewood housed one of Raphael's Madonna paintings known as *The Little Cowper Madonna*, while the gallery in the north wing displayed paintings by Van Eyck.

By 1941, Lynnewood Hall was no longer an art gallery, and in 1944 Joseph Widener passed away.

From his home at Lynnewood Hall on New Year's Eve, 1911, Harry wrote again to Luther Livingston about his Christmas holidays. "As far as news goes, I have very little to give you. We had a glorious Christmas and as usual I got several very fine books. Mother gave me three Keats volumes all in boards and all in the finest state. They were really fine and pleased me a great deal as I have wanted a fine set of Keats."

When attending sales such as the Robert Hoe sale in New York or the Huth sale in London, Harry would purchase volumes that he felt would be famous when better known and would delight the heart of a scholar. He also purchased volumes that had belonged to famous people, such as a rare Bible printed in 1550 that belonged to King Edward VI and Thackeray's *Henry Esmond* given with "grateful thanks" to Charlotte Brontë.

Harry Widener's knowledge of books, his familiarity with the chronicles of English literature, his enthusiasm, and his extraordinary memory, together with the interest and devotion of his grandfather and parents, enabled him to secure a collection of three thousand volumes in a short space of time. He was also fortunate in procuring the collaboration of Dr. Rosenbach and Bernard Quaritch.

***

Later Dr. Rosenbach would assist Harry in securing a catalog of his library to be of service to others. The catalog contained information and historical data that would prove of value to scholars. It was not a complete catalog, but a list of the choicest of his treasures: *A Catalogue of Some of the More Important Books, Manuscripts and Drawings in the Library of Harry Elkins Widener. Philadelphia Privately Printed 1910.* When Eleanor Elkins Widener created the library at Harvard in memory of her son, she asked Rosenbach for help in "building a collection worthy of his ambitions."

In a letter to A. C. R. Carter, a competent correspondent for the *Daily Telegraph* in London whose articles on book collecting, auctions, and personalities were considered outstanding, Bernard Quaritch said of Harry, "Perhaps it might interest you to know that Harry Elkins Widener who was drowned on the *Titanic* has left his Library to Harvard College … It includes the Van Antwerp and Locker Copy of the First folio. Should you care to see his Catalogue (privately printed quarto of 1910) I could lend it to you. Young Widener was only 26 and with his wealth, had he lived, he would no doubt have gathered one of the most remarkable libraries in America."

April 1912, London, England

So now Harry was about to say good-bye to his friend, Bernard Quaritch, take possession of that rare edition of Bacon's *Essaies* of 1598, and arrange for the disposition of his other purchases to be shipped on the RMS *Carpathia*.

With delicacy Harry took the book, spellbound and speechless. His eyes were drawn to the book as if it were a religious or sacred relic. It was a duodecimo-size, bound in black morocco gilt, and had a diamond-shaped motif on the front cover.

He read the words on the sleeve, "Bacon's Essaies, London 1598," and could not believe that he was actually holding it in his hand. Harry told Quaritch that he would take it with him as he didn't want to trust it with the other volumes he had bought. He would keep it in the dispatch box with which he always traveled. "I think I'll take that little Bacon with me in my pocket, and if I am shipwrecked it will go with me."

It is ironic that the RMS *Carpathia,* en route from New York to the Mediterranean at the time, picked up the disaster message from the *Titanic* and traveled northwest to the distressed liner.

CHAPTER 9

IDENTIFICATION PROCEDURES

April 17, 1912
Halifax, Nova Scotia

It was on a cool Wednesday, April 17, with a foggy breeze, that Dr. Jonathan Paul McKeebler, a surgeon and undertaker from Halifax, took out his pocket watch to make sure that he was on time for the departure of the first of the chartered ships, the *Mackay-Bennett*, for the harrowing job of searching for as many bodies as possible after the disaster in the Atlantic.

The *Mackay-Bennett* was built in Glasgow, Scotland, in 1845, fitted in London, and on February 17, 1885, cast off for Halifax, Nova Scotia. It was a 1,731-ton ship whose crew laid and repaired telecommunication cables linking Europe to the United States of America. Its name came from the business partnership of Mr. Mackay and Mr. Bennett, founders of the Commercial Cable Company in 1884. Mr. Bennett, a millionaire and entrepreneur, had financed Henry Stanley's expedition to Africa to discover Dr. Livingstone.

Mrs. Mackay had christened the ship and had also designed a large, mahogany-paneled cabin for her husband's use. On this occasion the cabin would be used by Reverend Gerard Hood.

On April 17, the *Mackay-Bennett* cast off from the wharf at Upper Water Street, Halifax and headed toward the last known position of the *Titanic*, which Jack Phillips, the Marconi wireless operator, had radioed before the ship went down. It would reach the scene within four days.

It carried over a hundred coffins, wooden cases of flasks containing embalming fluid, sheets of canvas for the second-class passengers, and ten tons of grate iron to weigh down the bodies to be buried at sea.

Dr. McKeebler, a well-proportioned man in his mid- to late forties, six feet tall, neatly dressed, with striking features, greeted Reverend Gerard Hood and Captain Frederick H. Larnder and boarded the vessel. Originally an undertaker and now an eminent surgeon, Dr. McKeebler had mixed feelings of apprehension and excitement at the thought of being part of a historical event. At the same time, he wondered how long he would be away from his wife and family and what decisions would have to be made concerning the bodies they would retrieve from the icy waters.

After a few days, it was clear that there were more bodies than had been expected. Many of the victims were still grouped together, which he thought might make it easier to recover the bodies. They were floating among the miles of wreckage, decking, tables, chairs, and luxury items, and were wearing cork life jackets that would keep them afloat for hours.

Captain Larnder, English by birth and accent, tall square build, with a full brown beard and eyes of unusual keenness, described the scene as "like nothing so much as a flock of seagulls resting on the water … All we could see at first would be the top of the life preservers. They were all floating face upward, apparently standing in the water."

Captain Larnder had been master of the *Mackay-Bennett* for five years. The Halifax *Evening Echo* published a picture of the ship with this report: "In the *Mackay-Bennett* the White Star Line have secured a ship specially well fitted for the task set her. Her commander, F. H. Larnder, is a thoroughly trained navigator, careful, and resourceful, and he has under his command a crew of officers and men that might be classed as picked."

"Some may have to be committed to the sea," McKeebler said to Reverend Hood as he looked at the bodies laid out on the deck.

"How long can we carry the dead? We have just over a hundred coffins. There's only enough embalming fluid for about seventy-five, and just a hundred tons of ice too," he said as he continued to check his inventory.

Reverend Gerard Francis Hood was a middle-aged clergyman from an Anglican church in Halifax. This quiet, unassuming gentleman of short, stocky appearance, with pince-nez glasses, was on board to administer to the dead and to conduct the services for any burial at sea. Those who could not be identified, whether by personal effects such as pocket contents, clothing, letters, tickets or initials on clothing, or those who could not be embalmed due to injuries received in the sinking were committed to the deep.

The captain and Reverend Hood spent most of the night repeating the words, "For as much as it pleaseth God … we therefore commit his body to the deep." Then would come the eerie sound of splash after splash as each body was plunged into the sea to sink to a depth of over a mile.

Each time wreckage and bodies were sighted, the ship's cutters were dispatched over the side. A watch was maintained from the bridge. Flags and whistles were used to direct the cutters to the bodies.

Dr. McKeebler gave instructions to the sailors that the bodies of crew members should be put in the ice-filled hold. Steerage and second-class passengers were sewn into canvas bags, and first-class passengers placed in coffins. The bodies were then transferred to portable embalming tables made of woven cane. A headrest supported the victim's head during the embalming process.

"Please arrange for the carpenters to build three screens so that I have some privacy and give some dignity to the deceased," demanded Dr. McKeebler as he searched each body for some identification.

They were classified in death as in life; social strata were adhered to even in death. It would only be in the cemeteries that bodies would be laid side by side, irrespective of whether they were first-, second-, or third-class passengers or crew.

The sight of forty bodies in a heap on the deck after they had been taken from the ice-filled hold was harrowing for all the volunteers, some of them only sixteen or seventeen years of age. They had to break some of the victims' frozen limbs in order to get them onto the stretchers and later into the coffins.

"How long do we have to continue this grim work?" asked William, one of the doctor's assistants. "I'm frozen."

"*You're* frozen?" riposted the doctor. "Just think of the volunteers in those awkward, heavy lifeboats in the cold with inadequate clothing—and with this large swell. It is hard enough to pull a live body from the sea, let alone a half-frozen deadweight."

"Yes, sir. I'm sorry. I was just caught off guard seeing the bodies of women and children."

"I understand, son," replied Dr. McKeebler, giving him a reassuring pat on the back. He realized that this volunteer could not be more than sixteen years of age and had never experienced such a situation. He tried to reassure him. "As one of the other sailors once said, the first ten bodies are the worst. After that it's just work, and you stop seeing bodies as people. Now, go and help with the identification procedures and then ask Reverend Hood about the burials at sea. He will need a hand with the grate iron. These bodies are so disfigured from the sinking and sea life that physical identification is impossible."

The day drew to its close. Reverend Hood had recommitted most bodies to the sea, wrapped in canvas sheeting and weighed down with the grate iron. The remaining bodies were embalmed and placed in coffins.

This became the daily, dreary routine. Each body was numbered sequentially as it was brought up to the rail and then lifted carefully and reverently to the deck.

The number was logged and stenciled on a piece of canvas, which was tied to the body. Personal effects and valuables were placed in small bags made from sailcloth and stenciled with the same number. This identification mark would follow the person through all the records and on to the photograph taken of each unidentified corpse. The bodies would be taken to the Mayflower Curling Rink, which was being made into a temporary mortuary ashore for when the *Mackay-Bennett* returned. All the bodies brought ashore were embalmed. A qualified female embalmer was drafted in especially for the women and children. Many of the bodies would have been identified by the contents of their pockets or clothing.

"Just one more body to record. Then we're through for today." Dr. McKeebler sighed, stretched, and yawned. "William, can you come and help me, please?" he called to one of his assistants. "This is body number forty-five."

William took out his pen and wrote, "Identification number forty-five."

There was a letter in the body's coat pocket addressed to George Widener. At first they thought it was the body of George Widener, Harry's father, but it was only later, after careful screening of the coat and garments and seeing the label EK, that he was identified as Edwin Keeping, George Widener's valet.

A week passed. There had been delays because of the fog. The sea was calm, the light was beginning to fade, and the ship's cutters were concluding their recovery operations when there came a shout from one of the sailors on deck of the *Mackay-Bennett.*

"Look over there. About twelve o'clock, where the sun is setting! There's something reflecting in the water bobbing about. It looks like a jacket." He paused. "No, I think it is a body. Before you tie up and come on board, can you confirm?"

"Okay. We'll take a look," replied one of the crew.

The cutter proceeded toward the object, and within an hour they had retrieved this lost soul.

The body was lifted up to the ship's rail and laid on the deck. Once again, as with so many bodies, the methodical identification process began.

Dr. McKeebler began the formalities by searching through the pockets of the clothing and recording his findings. "Identification number 223. Body, male youth, approximately twenty-seven years old. Dark hair, straight, crystallized central parting. Clothing, seaman's peacoat over fashionable clothing. Demeanor peaceful. Right hand clasped to left breast."

An eerie feeling came over him as his warm hand prized the stiff, half-frozen right hand from its position. He noticed a bulge from the inside pocket and found something wrapped in what appeared to be a silk handkerchief. He knew that many of the crew had helped themselves to valuables and dressed themselves in Savile Row suits or fur coats. Unwrapping the silk, he saw that it covered a book and figured that the sailor had taken it from the cabin of a first-class passenger.

He continued searching in the hope of finding some form of identification, but there was only a mixture of American, French, and British coins in the pockets, which puzzled him. He also found a pocket watch, chain, and fob. There being no other form of identification, he finalized his official list: "Effects: pocket watch, chain, and fob. American, French, and British coins. No other ID. Identification number 223."

It was usual to put crew members in the ice-filled hold. But, as this was the last body of the day, Dr. McKeebler sent his assistant undertaker to fetch one of the canvas bags usually reserved for steerage and second-class passengers.

As he was putting the coins into the canvas bag, he realized that he had omitted making a record of the book and handkerchief, which he had put aside in order to search for any possible trace of identity. He unwrapped the handkerchief from the book. On a closer look at the book, which had suffered badly from immersion in water, he could just make out the title on the spine:

Bacon's Essaies
London
1598

Himself a bibliophile and an avid collector of books, he knew that the author was Francis Bacon and, by the date, that it was one of the earliest editions of this work. Excitement filled him and his heart began to pound. The desire for possession of the book compromised his morality, and his primal instinct took over. He *had* to have it. He rewrapped the book in the handkerchief, placed it inside his own jacket, and gave the matter no further thought.

From a distance he heard the ship's bell toll to indicated that a burial service was about to begin. He stared at the starry heavens in the solemn stillness of the night as the customary words of the service taking place on deck once again rang out. "I am the resurrection and the life … We therefore commit his body to the deep, looking for the resurrection of the body when the seas shall give up her dead."

News came through that the *Mackay-Bennett* would be returning to Halifax, and that the *Minia* would continue the task. Dr. McKeebler retired to his cabin to take his tot of rum and then settle down for a good night's sleep. As he removed his jacket, he felt the book in his own inside pocket. In the bustle, he had forgotten it. He removed the silk handkerchief, uncovered the book, and carefully leafed through a few pages in amazement. He put it on the nightstand to dry out, excited at the thought of this newly acquired possession. However, the feeling was tainted by his impropriety.

He knew that the 1625 final edition of Bacon's *Essaies* comprised fifty-eight essays. This book had just ten, which gave further credence to it being a rare edition.

He climbed into his bed and kissed the grainy photograph of his wife, Madeleine, and his children, Jerome and Katarina, which he always carried with him. It would only be a few days and they would be reunited again. He mused over the last body of the day, number 223, and pondered on the position of the sailor's half-frozen right hand. *Had he been clasping the book when he jumped? Why and how did he get the book?*

McKeebler also wrestled with his conscience about removing the book from the sailor, which was counterbalanced by the fact that the sailor had no further use for it.

Sleep soon relieved him from the fatigue of the day's overwhelming activities and the physical and emotional strain of the past weeks. The day's events leafed through his mind like snapshots in a photo album. As he slept, a repeat of the day's events manifested themselves in a dream. The process of finding some identification, his hand sliding toward the bulge in the sailor's peacoat, the book. He felt the touch of a cool, damp, restricting hand on his and abruptly woke up. Frightened, he reached over to turn on the light and knocked the book to the floor. The page opened at the essay "Of Honour and Reputation." He was shaking. Perspiration ran down his face in spite of the cold cabin.

He recalled his dream of the identification process for that last body—the unclasping of the frosted hand, the removal of the peacoat, the coins, the moment he removed the bulge from the man's pocket. His own heartbeat deceived him into thinking that he could hear the ticking of the pocket watch. *Was this a parallelism?* A cacophony of bells ringing, voices, and shouting from the crew conjured up this kaleidoscope of images. It felt so factual that he was disturbed, unsettled, and distracted.

On Tuesday, April 30, the *Mackay-Bennett,* which saw the worst of the tragedy and was therefore called "the death ship," returned to Halifax, having recovered 306 bodies, of which 116 were buried at sea. President Mackay wired Captain Larnder, "In appreciation of the efficient services of yourself and your officers and crew of over one hundred men, in a work humanitarian and yet entirely outside of your regular line of duty, the Commercial Cable Company allows you and your officers and men double pay for the time engaged."

As Jay Henry Mowbray wrote, "What seems a very regrettable fact is that in chartering the *Mackay-Bennett* for this work the White Star Company did not send an officer agent to accompany the steamer in her search for the bodies."

Due to the coast mist hanging over the sea, the lookout on Citadel Hill had difficulty seeing the mouth of the harbor, let alone the *Mackay-Bennett.* Just after eight o'clock in the morning he made out the outline of a ship and hoisted the black flag. This was the agreed signal to alert those waiting on the pier.

At nine o'clock, the quarantine boat *Monica* and the tugboat *Scotsman* intercepted the *Mackay-Bennett*, and Dr. McKeebler fulfilled the necessary legal requirements for the ship to enter the harbor.

The vessel tied up at nine thirty on Coaling Jetty 4 at the flagship pier amid the security of H. M. Dockyard in Halifax, where all in attendance were silent with heads bare. Flags were flown at half-mast. The cathedral bell was the first to ring out, followed by the bells of more than forty churches in Halifax.

The initial shock to the people waiting on the shore upon seeing the *Mackay-Bennett* was devastating. The *New York Times* reported, "Some fainted and fell while others just turned away."

The bodies were taken ashore, which took over three and a half hours, and laid out in the Mayflower Curling Rink on the edge of the town.

The following day, Dr. McKeebler called in more embalmers, as there were relatives already waiting to claim the bodies of those identified. The medical examiner issued little crimson tickets as the death certificates, and the registrar issued the burial permits.

The first body that was identified, claimed, and removed from the Mayflower Rink was John Jacob Astor, age forty-seven, of 840 Fifth Avenue, New York City. Vincent, his son, and Nicholas Briddle, his lawyer and trustee of the Astor estate, returned the body to New York the next night. The second body was that of Isidor Straus, founder of the world-famous Macy's department store in New York.

Meanwhile, Reverend Gerard Hood was arranging memorial services and comforting the bereaved. Most of the victims were buried between May 3 and June 12. Individuals donated flowers, and unidentified graves were adorned with bouquets of lilies. The majority of the gravestones were erected in the fall of 1912.

For the captain of the *Mackay-Bennett*, the crew, the sailors on the cutters, Dr. McKeebler, and Reverend Hood, the agonizing ordeal was over, but the nightmares and the recurrent flashbacks were just beginning. The story would be told to their children and their children's children.

Dr. McKeebler made his way to his home on Young Avenue. As he reached the corner of Inglis Street, he noticed a large gathering of people outside 989 Young Street, the mansion of George Wright. Wright had designed and built it for himself in 1902. George was McKeebler's friend and neighbor, a prominent member of Halifax society and a self-made millionaire. He was instrumental in bringing the people of Halifax together and tried to minimize the divide between rich and poor. Coincidentally he was the only person from Halifax to lose his life on the *Titanic*. On April 20, the headline in the Halifax *Herald* noted, "Halifax loses a good man in Geo. Wright."

Dr. McKeebler hurried past with his head down, shocked that someone he had known for years had lost his life in the tragedy. The bodies he had either identified or embalmed had been unknown to him, and that had been his job. Here was reality.

Nervously he approached his own front gate and hesitated as he took in his surroundings. In just a few weeks his world had been turned upside down. Now he was returning to his familiar environment.

He entered the house and was enthusiastically greeted by his wife and children. He was exhausted physically and mentally, so, after a few minutes of platitudes, he retired to his room to rest. He just wanted some quiet and solitude, and assured Madeleine and the children that he would see them at dinner.

Jerome, age ten, went into the garden to play soccer with his friends, but Katarina, age seven, just wanted her daddy and couldn't understand what was wrong.

After a few hours, Madeleine went upstairs to call him for dinner. When she found him in what she thought was a deep sleep, she did not disturb him. He was not actually sleeping but reliving the finding of the bodies, the embalming, the burials, and, more importantly, the book that he had taken from body 223.

The following day, he took the book from his briefcase, removed the silk handkerchief, took a lingering look at it, and then wrapped it neatly and placed it in his safe in the library. Each day he would retire to the library after dinner, making it clear that he did not want to be disturbed, look at the Bacon, and replace it in the safe.

Although Madeleine had noticed that he had become noncommunicative, withdrawn, impatient with the children, and restless, she thought it was due to his experiences. She convinced herself that he would come out of it in a few days.

CHAPTER 10

HARRY ELKINS WIDENER'S FATAL VOYAGE

Wednesday, April 10, 1912

Harry Elkins Widener, his parents George and Eleanor, Edwin Keeping, the valet, and Amalie Gieger, Eleanor's maid, left the Gare St. Lazare in Paris at 9:40 a.m. They arrived at the transatlantic railway terminal of the New York express train in Cherbourg six hours later. Cherbourg was the gateway for an increasing number of wealthy Americans to travel throughout Europe.

It was here that they were informed that the *Titanic* had been involved in a near collision with the *New York*, and there would be a delay of about an hour.

At five o'clock, the small White Star steamship the *Nomadic* began transferring the first- and second-class passengers and their carefully labeled luggage to the great ship. A second steamship, the *Traffic*, picked up the third-class passengers.

At 6:35 p.m., they watched excitedly as the magnificent liner, all lit up against the different hues of blue of the ocean and sky, dropped anchor in the great roadstead of Cherbourg. After half an hour, the Widener party embarked on the *Titanic*. By eight o'clock all the passengers were on board and the tenders returned to the shore. At 8:10 p.m., the *Titanic* departed for Queenstown on the south coast of County Cork in Ireland.

"Be careful with that trunk," shouted Edwin. "That is Mrs. Widener's daughter's trousseau."

As they arrived, the steward showed George and Eleanor Widener to stateroom 80 and Harry to stateroom 82, both located on C deck, which was one of the decks reserved for the first-class passengers. Eleanor Widener handed her expensive jewelry to the purser to be locked away in the safe. He pointed out the green mesh bag for watches, hanging on the wall next to the bed.

"This is much more spacious and lavish than the *Mauretania*," remarked Amalie to Edwin as they began unpacking the vast quantities of belongings from the steamer trunks.

"Two bedrooms, a sitting room, two dressing rooms, and a private bathroom!" he exclaimed.

"The two dressing rooms will be so useful. They'll be changing their clothes every five minutes!" responded Amalie.

Meanwhile Harry was settling in his cabin, carefully taking the Bacon from his tin-lined dispatch box and placing it on his nightstand. When his mother entered, he pointed it out to her. "Hello, Mother. Isn't it wonderful? I shall be able to read quietly in here as well as take advantage of the library during the voyage."

"Yes, it is wonderful," she replied, getting a little agitated. "Harry, it's getting late. I came to tell you that we'll be gathering for cocktails in the reception room in about half an hour. We've decided to eat in the first-class dining saloon, as the quintet will be playing there tonight."

The quintet, led by the violinist Wallace Hartley, played at teatime, after dinner, and at Sunday services. The violin, cello, and piano trio played at the à la carte restaurant and the Café Parisienne.

"Excellent," replied Harry. "I remember Wallace Hartley from the *Mauretania*. It will be good to see him again. Anyway, I look forward to seeing you later in one of your new Parisian gowns, Mother."

The reception room was simple in decor, with white paneling delicately carved in low relief. The first-class dining saloon, on the other hand, occupied the whole length of the ship and was the largest room afloat. As the diners waited for the doors to open, they could admire an Aubusson tapestry depicting a medieval hunting scene and listen to the mellifluous tones of the orchestra.

The seven-course evening meal was the social highlight of the day. When they had finished, Harry withdrew to the smoking lounge and looked around at the stained-glass windows and mother-of-pearl-inlaid mahogany paneling. Hung above the fireplace was a painting by Norman Wilkinson entitled *Approach to Plymouth.*

Harry chatted briefly with Frank Millet, the well-known Washington artist who specialized in mural decoration, about their love and ambition for Harvard University. Later he joined his father and his friends in one of the green leather chairs grouped around a small table and began reading his latest acquisition—Bacon's *Essaies.*

One of the party, William Carter, a fine horseman from Philadelphia who divided his time between Europe and America, asked, "Would you like a cigar, Harry?"

"No, thanks," he replied, looking up from his book. "I'm just going to finish my cordial and take a stroll on deck before I run into the stewards taking those highly strung dogs for a walk. I don't want another encounter with that French bulldog! Also, I have some letters to write, and I want to read my new book. It's a copy of the 1598 *Essaies* by Francis Bacon which I have just purchased from my friend in London."

"I thought Bacon was an English statesman and philosopher, not a writer," William said, tapping his cigar on the ashtray.

"True," replied Harry, anxious to share his enthusiasm with William. "He was known as Baron Verulam or, as the English called him, Viscount St. Albans. He was renowned as a scientist and a scholar as well as a statesman. In his own words, he 'regarded the world as a puzzle to be solved.' Anyway, he also wrote essays that had a great influence on seventeenth-century Europe. My book contains ten essays. You see, it is a rare second edition. Here, take a look at this. 'Of Friendship,'" he said, somewhat reluctantly handing his treasured book over.

William took the little book and read aloud, "A principal fruit of friendship is the ease and discharge of the fulness and swellings of the heart, which passions of all kinds do cause and induce."

"Now look at this page, 'Of Studies,'" continued Harry, looking over William's shoulder. He quoted, "'Read not to contradict and confute; nor to believe and take for granted; nor to find talk and discourse, but to weigh and consider. Some books are to be tasted, others to be swallowed and some few to be chewed and digested.' And look here: 'Reading maketh the full man.' That is what it is all about. That is what I am about."

"Were these essays based on his own experience?"

"Yes. He didn't actually intend the essays to be published but just wanted to share some personal notes with his friends," Harry replied, sensitively taking the book back into his hands. "They were received with such enthusiasm that his friends suggested that they be published. Remarkable, isn't it? Well, if you'll excuse me, I'll say good night. It has been nice talking with you and sharing one of my passions."

"When we return home, you must share in one of my preoccupations—my new Renault automobile! You'll also have to try your hand at polo when we return. Good night, Harry."

Angus MacDade, a Scottish aristocrat, who was sitting at the adjacent card table, had heard some of the conversation. He approached Harry as he was getting up from his seat. "Excuse me, sir. I couldn't help overhearing your conversation and noting your exuberance about your new book purchase. It appears that we have a great deal in common and that you have as much passion for books as I do. May I introduce myself? The name's Angus. Angus MacDade."

"My name's Harry. Harry Elkins Widener," he replied, shaking MacDade's hand. "I am pleased to make your acquaintance."

Angus said, "I have just acquired a rare first Edinburgh edition of Robert Burns's *Poems Chiefly in the Scottish Dialect—1787*, which contains the misprint 'Duke of Boxburgh' for Roxburgh!"

"How wonderful! How is it bound?" inquired Harry.

"In purple crushed morocco. Also, Bernard Quaritch secured the first London edition of the same, which succeeds the Edinburgh edition. That is bound in green crushed morocco, spine lettered, and dated in gilt raised bands. An exceptional purchase, do you not agree?"

"Yes, indeed. What a coincidence! Bernard Quaritch is a great friend of mine, and I too have purchased many books from him over the years. In fact, my other recent purchases are being sent home on the *Carpathia*. I have only the Bacon with me. We must talk at greater length tomorrow."

"I shall look forward to that. Good night to you."

"What a charming fellow," said Angus to William as he signaled to the steward for another cordial.

"Yes," replied William. "He has many interests and excels at all of them. You would never guess that he stands to inherit Philadelphia's largest fortune. He's totally unassuming and unpretentious and never puts on airs of any sort."

"Fascinating. I'll look forward to continuing the discussion with him tomorrow. Now, would you like a wee dram before we retire?"

"No, thank you," replied William as he stood up to take his leave. "Then I'll bid you good night."

Thursday, April 11, 1912

Around noon the following day, the ship anchored two miles off the shore of Queenstown to drop off those passengers who were only traveling as far as Ireland and pick up more passengers including 123 Irish emigrants.

During that time Harry and his family took lunch in the first-class dining room, while other voyagers passed the time watching the two ageing White Star tenders arrive—the PS *Americ*a and PS *Ireland*—as well as several other smaller boats delivering the first-class luggage. More passengers strolled on the deck or went aft to look at the display of Irish lace, crystal, china, and other souvenirs set up by the merchants who had arrived on the bumboats.

The voyage was resumed at 1:40 p.m., signaled by three long blasts from *Titanic*'s whistle as she made her way toward the open sea.

Friday, April 12, 1912

It was a beautiful, calm day with a gentle sea breeze, and life on board continued. Harry rose early and visited his parents in the adjacent stateroom. The steward was already serving them with coffee and fruit.

"Good morning," he said, embracing his mother. "I've come to join you. It's such a glorious day, isn't it?"

"Good morning, Harry," replied his mother as she tidied her robe. "Steward, would you bring extra coffee for my son? What are you going to do today?" she asked, turning toward Harry.

"First I shall eat a generous breakfast. Then I think I'll just go and read my book on the boat deck. What about you?"

"Your father is going to play cards and socialize in the smoking room and then take a Turkish bath this afternoon, aren't you, George?"

George acknowledged her with a grunt as he continued reading his copy of the *Atlantic Daily Bulletin* that had just been brought in by the steward.

"I shall go to the wireless room and send a couple of messages. Then I'm meeting Marian Thayer and Emily Ryerson in the reception room before lunch."

"To talk about couture, no doubt," added George cynically as he peered over his paper.

"No, George," she replied firmly. "Emily lost her son in a car accident recently and is grieving. She has hardly left her stateroom since we sailed."

"I apologize for my insensitivity," replied George, putting his paper down.

"By the way, we are taking a late lunch today," she said, turning back to Harry. "William and Lucile Carter will be joining us and possibly John and Marian Thayer. I think Jack Junior will be lunching with young Lucile and Billy in their stateroom."

"Yes, Mother," replied Harry as he made his way toward the door. "I enjoy their company. What time?"

"We have arranged for two o'clock."

Harry took his leave and after taking breakfast went to the boat deck, where he found some other passengers contentedly lazing around on deck chairs, oblivious to the fact that the lifeboats hanging from the davits restricted their view of the sea. The steward moved Harry's deck chair some distance away and brought him a hot drink and a blanket. He settled down for a peaceful morning.

Suddenly Harry's concentration was interrupted by the noise of the children, who were playing deck quoits and shuffleboard and generally running around happily with their onboard friends. He returned to his cabin and took solace there until luncheon.

Saturday, April 13, 1912

Eleanor Elkins Widener chose the dinner menu and the seating arrangements for her guests with the restaurant manager Luigi Gatti and Chef Pierre Rousseau's personal assistant, the maître d' Paul Mougé. They decided on seven courses with a fresh glass of wine to complement each course.

"We'll have the plover eggs in aspic with caviar, and the Egyptian quail eggs, followed by the spring pea soup. For the fish course, we'll take the lobster thermidor. I assume this will be served in the traditional way, on a silver platter surrounded by duchesse potatoes?"

"Yes, madam. Of course."

"Excellent. Now the entrée. I think the tournedos. Do you have those luxurious morel mushrooms?"

"Yes, madam," Signor Gatti replied, taking copious notes. "Might I suggest the rosewater and mint sorbet, with the punch rosé to follow?"

"Of course. For the rôti, I think the quails with cherries would go down well, and spring asparagus, but not cooked for too long, with your rich hollandaise sauce."

"Yes, madam. Might I suggest peeled pears, peaches, and plums for the *Macédone des fruits*? These have been imported a great distance from exotic climes. I can also recommend the hothouse grapes."

"Thank you. Yes, that will be fine. You can give us the *oranges en surprise* for dessert."

"Thank you, madam. Leave everything to me."

Luigi Gatti was responsible for the complete administration of the restaurant, and all its employees were employed by him, not White Star. Most of his staff were drawn from his London Adelphi and Strand restaurants. Nothing was too much trouble for him, and every whim and wish was catered to.

Meanwhile the ship had covered 386 nautical miles since midday on Thursday. By Saturday, the total was 509 nautical miles.

CHAPTER 11

THE FOUNDERING OF RMS *TITANIC*

Sunday, April 14, 1912

At 9 o'clock on Sunday morning, Captain Smith posted a message on the bridge for his officers. It had come from the eastbound liner *Caronia*, notifying him of "bergs, growlers, and field ice." Just over two hours later, the *Nordam* also reported much ice in the same place.

Meanwhile, Colonel Archibald Gracie had played a game of squash with the ship's pro, Fred Wright, taken a dip in the pool, changed into his blue blazer, and eaten a hearty breakfast. He was on his way back to his stateroom when he saw Captain Smith.

"Are we having a lifeboat drill this morning?" he asked.

"Not today. I've canceled it due to the strong breeze," the captain replied. He continued on his way to make preparations for the church service that he was due to lead in the first-class dining room.

More wireless warnings came in during the afternoon. The Cunarder *Baltic* liner reported ice 250 miles away at 1:42 p.m. Only three minutes later, yet another warning came in. Captain Smith took the message from the *Baltic* down to lunch to show his officers. En route, he met J. Bruce Ismay, chairman and managing director of the White Star Line, who was in conversation with George and Eleanor Widener.

"I've just received this telegram that we are in the midst of icebergs," he said as he pulled the telegram from his pocket. "I'm on my way to speak with my officers."

"Do you think it's serious?" Ismay asked.

"No, I don't think so."

Later that afternoon, Mrs. Ryerson and Mrs. Thayer were sitting on deck, watching the sunset. The captain greeted them. "Good evening, ladies. Isn't this a magnificent sunset? You wouldn't believe that we are near the icebergs."

"Is it going to be dangerous?" asked Mrs. Thayer.

"I'm not too worried. Rest assured that the ship will arrive ahead of schedule in New York. Good evening to you both," he said, touching his forehead in acknowledgment.

A lavish dinner party was being hosted by the Wideners in honor of Captain Edward J. Smith, whose distinguished career was ending with his last voyage—the maiden voyage of the *Titanic*. The dinner was to be held in the à la carte restaurant situated on B deck. It was also known as the Ritz Restaurant because of its imitation of the fashionable Ritz-Carlton restaurants and the culinary standards that had been set by César Ritz himself. The service was similar to that of the White Star Line's German rivals—the Hamburg-American Line.

The restaurant was opened from eight o'clock to eleven o'clock in the evening, and could be reserved for private parties as well. It provided a forum for Chef Rousseau to show off his culinary skills. The menu comprised many courses freshly prepared and in considerable quantity, all served with excellent wines. It was an addition to the already sumptuous first-class dining saloon. The rich and famous queued up for the privilege of dining at the Ritz and were given a reduction on their fare by White Star for dining there.

The restaurant was decorated in Louis XIV Seize style with French walnut paneling and furniture. There were starched white linen tablecloths and napkins that set off the sparkling glassware and Royal Crown Derby china delicately trimmed in gold with green garland. The polished silverware, cutlery, and condiments had plain, long-fluted stems with the insignia of the White Star Line. Each table was garlanded with pink roses and white daisies.

The Wideners had invited grandees and sought-after dining companions John and Marian Thayer and William and Lucile Carter. John Thayer was second vice president of the Pennsylvania Railroad and had inherited most of his wealth, whereas William Carter's income had been enhanced by his marriage to the daughter of the eleventh president of the United States, James Knox Polk. Other guests were Major Archibald Butt, an influential military aide to US presidents Theodore Roosevelt and William Howard Taft; and Clarence Moore, a Washington banker with the firm William B. Hibbs and Co. He served as master of hounds at the exclusive Chevy Chase Hunt Club. He had traveled to the north of England to purchase twenty-five brace of foxhounds from the best packs for the Loudon Hunt. He had also been involved, along with a newspaper reporter, in interviewing Captain Anse Hatfield of the famous Hatfield and McCoy family dispute.

That Evening

The Wideners and their guests gathered at seven thirty in the reception room. A long table expanded into an alcove separated by the carved paneling near the entrance. Captain Smith was seated at the head of the table with Eleanor Widener on his right and Archibald Butt on his left. It was an exciting evening. The ladies had dressed in their new silk and satin Parisian gowns and wore their most sparkling jewels for the first time. Eleanor Widener was concerned that Lucile Thayer's attire would be unconventional, as Lucile had been the first woman in Philadelphia to wear a harem skirt. Eleanor wondered what she had acquired from Paris.

Captain Smith was gossiping about the ship and boasting of its splendor. He received the adulation of the ladies regarding his distinguished career. He was a bearded father figure worshipped by crew and passengers alike. He had been described as "a natural leader with that rare combination of firmness and urbanity."

"There is some speculation about icebergs," commented Mrs. Thayer.

"No need to worry," Captain Smith assured her. "My crew is taking care of the necessary precautions. There will be no need to change speed at this time. The night is clear, so the lookout will spot any iceberg early."

Major Butt, Marian Thayer, and Eleanor Widener were engaged in conversation on different topics. Clarence Moore was relating tales of his adventures in the mountains and forests of West Virginia, while Harry Widener was talking about financial matters with William Carter. Marian Thayer and Archibald Butt became engrossed in one another, mutually opening up their hearts, leaving Eleanor Widener to entertain Captain Smith.

At 8:30 p.m., the Wideners and their guests had coffee in the reception room, while outside the dining saloon, the orchestra played tunes by Puccini and other operetta composers. Archibald Butt continued to be engaged in conversation with Marian Thayer and expressed his anxiety about returning home. At eleven thirty, the lounge had emptied and only the public rooms were open. Harry,

Colonel Gracie, Clarence Moore, and William Carter retired to the smoking lounge for a nightcap and played bridge and whist until most of the other passengers had gone to bed.

Captain Smith had returned to the bridge at 8:55 p.m. "There's no need to slow down unless it becomes hazy," he said to Second Officer Charles Lightoller. "There's little wind, and the sea is smooth and calm. It has turned really cold, hasn't it?" He scanned the bridge.

"It's only one degree above freezing," Lightoller replied. "It is unfortunate that we shall be unable to see the waves breaking on any icebergs."

"If there is any problem, then please let me know. I shall be in my cabin if you need me."

The Final Hours

At 11:40 p.m., there was a sudden, dreadful shuddering, followed by a rumble, a roar, and a general commotion. What was going on? An eyewitness told of an iceberg rising over a hundred feet above the water. That meant it extended about five hundred feet below the surface.

John Thayer, second vice president of the Pennsylvania Railroad, and his wife, Marian, were traveling with their seventeen-year-old son, Jack. John and Marian had joined the Wideners for dinner and were going to bed when the collision occurred. Jack was in his pajamas in his stateroom on B deck when he heard the hum of the breeze suddenly stop. He went to investigate and saw some ice on the forward deck.

"Mother, Father, come quickly. There's ice on the deck. Look at those boys playing with it."

His parents joined him on deck and noticed that the ship had a slight list to the port side.

It wasn't until the stateroom stewards came on duty at twelve thirty, knocking on cabin doors to rouse the passengers and instructing other passengers on deck and in the lounges, that the Thayers realized the seriousness of the situation.

"All back to your staterooms for your life preservers and warm clothing to combat the icy conditions," the stewards cried.

There wasn't much panic, just confusion. There were no bells, no sirens, no general alarm. Some people even thought that this was a drill and refused to leave the warmth of their cabins for such an inconvenient and inconsiderate exercise. The band was playing lively tunes, and others headed to the bar for a stiff drink. No one in the first-class smoking lounge seemed to know what was occurring. The bridge game continued in full swing.

"We must return to the stateroom and put on some warm clothes," Marian Thayer urged them.

"What's going on?" asked one of the passengers who had come out of his stateroom. "I'm trying to dictate a letter. What's all the noise and commotion?"

Mrs. Ryerson looked out of her cabin and, on seeing a steward, asked, "Why have the engines stopped?"

The steward explained, "There's talk of an iceberg, ma'am, and they've stopped so as not to run it over."

She wondered what to do. Her husband was having his first good sleep since the start of the trip, and she hated to wake him. As she looked out on deck, all she saw was a beautiful, clear, calm night. The decision seemed made for her; she let him sleep on.

Meanwhile, there was much turmoil as First Officer Murdoch on the starboard side with the odd-numbered lifeboats stipulated,

"Women and children first," while Second Officer Lightoller on the port side said, "Women and children only."

The evacuation process broke families apart. There were people running everywhere without direction. Crowds began to gather in the lounges and the foyers while others fought their way to the purser's office to claim their valuables.

Colonel Gracie bumped into Fred Wright, the *Titanic*'s squash pro. "You know that we have a court booked for tomorrow at seven thirty? I think we might have to cancel that appointment."

"Yes, I agree," replied Wright as he continued on his way.

Colonel Gracie did not realize the severity of the incident at the time, but Fred had appeared concerned, probably because by that time he knew that the racquet court was filling up with water.

Fred was last seen smoking a cigarette before the ship sank. Sadly, his body was never found.

Many of the women would not be parted from their loved ones. It was reported that the women millionaires were patient, showed good manners, waited anxiously and proudly, and did not insist on privileges. Although lifeboat 4 was the first one ready on the port side, it was last to leave. Lightoller had been asked to fill it from the promenade deck, but Captain Smith had forgotten that the deck was protected from the wind by glass windows known as Ismay screens. Therefore the women and children had returned to the boat deck as lifeboat 4 was lowered outside the promenade deck.

Deck chairs were stacked, and Lightoller, John Astor, and John Thayer helped the women and children board. The New York and Philadelphia society passengers either stood or paced the deck, waiting patiently to board a lifeboat. The forward part of the deck was the promenade space for the first-class passengers, and the rear part was for second-class. They had the best chance of getting into a lifeboat as they were in easy reach.

John and Jack Thayer said good-bye to Marian at the top of the grand staircase and then saw her and two of her children into lifeboat 4.

Eleanor Widener was one of the last women of that group to leave the ship. She kissed George and Harry good-bye on deck, supposing that the parting would only be for a short time. They had no thought that the *Titanic* would sink. When the realization set in, she began screaming uncontrollably as she fought to die with her husband and son. She probably would have succeeded had it not been for a couple of seamen who literally tore her from her husband and forced her into the lifeboat. Her frantic, despairing pleas to remain with her husband and son were overshadowed by George's cries: "Go! Go! For God's sake, go, Nellie. You take the first ship to New York and we'll follow." He then called out to Amalie Gieger, Eleanor's maid, and Marian Thayer, who were already in the boat, "Take care of her."

Turning back to his wife, he said, "Nellie, dearest, remember what I have always said. Promise me that nothing will interfere with the plans of the family. Whatever happens, Eleanor and Eugene's wedding will go ahead on the appointed day."

Her pitiful wails continued as she descended the ladder, "Oh my God!" she cried. "Good-bye! Good-bye! George! Harry! Good-bye. Oh my God, this is awful!"

Harry looked on in pain. As he said good-bye to his mother, he was reputed to have said, "Mother, I have placed the little Bacon in my pocket. The little Bacon goes with me."

That was the last she saw of her husband and son, who waved a brave farewell as she disappeared into the boat. Soon the boat touched the water and they were rowed out to sea.

William Carter had also said good-bye to his wife and children and watched them go into the boat. One of the most interesting statements made by Mr. Carter after the sinking was "that a short time before he left the ship he spoke to Harry E. Widener and advised him to get into one of the boats if he could. Mr. Widener replied: 'I think I'll stick to the big ship, Billy, and take a chance.'"

Relating his experiences, Mr. Carter said:

> I was in the smoking room for several hours prior to the collision with Major Archie Butt, Colonel Gracie, Harry Widener, Mr. Thayer, Clarence Moore, of Washington, William Dulles, and several other men.
>
> At exactly seventeen minutes to 12 o'clock we felt a jar and left the room to see what the trouble was outside. We were told that the ship had struck an iceberg. Many of the men were in the card room, and after learning what had happened returned to their games.
>
> The officers informed us that the accident was not a serious one, and there was little excitement at the time. However, I went to the lower deck, where Mrs. Carter and my two children were sleeping. I awoke my wife and told her what had occurred and advised her to dress and take the children to the deck.
>
> I then returned to the upper deck and found that the crew was lowering lifeboats containing women and children. When Mrs. Carter and the children came up I had them placed in one of the boats,

> which also contained Mrs. Astor, Mrs. Widener, Mrs. Thayer, and several other women.

Water Pouring into the Ship

> I believed at the time that they would all return to the steamer in a short time, feeling certain that there was no danger. A few minutes later, however, I learned that water was pouring into the ship and that she was in a serious condition. I saw Harry Widener and walked to where he was standing on the port side of the Titanic. An order had been given before the boats were launched to put on lifebelts, and I had adjusted one around myself.
>
> I said to Mr. Widener, "Come on, Harry, let us go to the starboard side and see if there is any chance to get in one of the boats." He replied, "I think I'll stick to the big ship, Billy, and take a chance." I left him there and went to the starboard side of A deck.
>
> George, Harry, John Thayer, and J. J. Astor remained together by the midship rail while Benjamin Guggenheim and his valet changed into evening dress as they said that they "were prepared to go down like gentlemen."

George and Harry Widener thought that lifeboat 4 had left, but there had been a delay in launching it. In fact, it eventually left at 1:50 a.m. and was one of the last to leave.

According to George McGough, a buyer for Gimbels department store, George and Harry Widener remained calm, helping women and children to make their escape, and stood back as the boats and craft were launched. They seemed to be resigned to the fact that they had lived well and so would die well. The *Philadelphia Inquirer*, under the headline "Widener and Son Met Heroic Death When Titanic Sank," wrote, "Financier, as Calm as Though taking a Walk on Broad Street, Stood back With Harry Elkins Widener That Weaker Might Be Rescued—Wife, Now at Home Here, Clung to Husband Until Sailors Tore Her From him."

They would later publish, "George D. Widener and his son, Harry Elkins Widener, lost in the wreck of the *Titanic*, died the death of heroes. They stood back that the weaker might have a chance of being saved."

Some of the male passengers leaned over the side of the deck for a last, lingering look at the faces of their wives and children before they became indistinguishable in the darkness. Passengers mingling together made a kaleidoscope of fashion—bathrobes, evening attire, fur coats, sweaters. There was last-minute conveyance of personal items from passengers in the lifeboats.

Meanwhile, Jack Thayer and a shipboard acquaintance named Milton Long, whom he had met over coffee that evening, found themselves separated from John and Marian Thayer on A deck. Suddenly they saw a large wave approaching and, instead of making for a higher point, decided to jump and swim for it. They stood by the starboard rail opposite the second funnel. They shook hands, exchanged messages for their families, and wished each other luck. Jack Thayer was picked up by lifeboat 12. Milton Long was not seen again.

As collapsible lifeboat C was lowered at 1:40 a.m., J. Bruce Ismay and William Carter climbed in. William Carter and his family would be the only complete family from the dinner party to survive. Maître d' Paul Mougé also survived. Death was now the divider of families.

As the blinding flashes from the rockets rose into the clear night sky like a trail of stars, Harry realized that the *Titanic* was in real danger.

About one fifteen, without warning or reason, Harry left his father to return to his stateroom. "Father, I'll be right back. I have to clear my head, and I'm so cold."

Harry's body seemed to be producing some kind of drug similar to the effects of opium. He felt almost nothing. Numbness surpassed pain and fear, and he felt no control over his body. He thought of all the good times and the pleasures that he would never enjoy. He felt far away, as if he were looking on from a distant place, similar to an out-of-body experience. He became oblivious to the shouting, the noise, and the strains of the band, who had been instructed to play music to maintain calm while people were waiting in line for the lifeboats.

Then all became silent.

The steps didn't seem quite right. They appeared to be level, but his feet fell forward as though the steps were tilting toward the bow. He finally reached his stateroom on C deck.

"Excuse me, sir; you cannot return here," said the steward. "I have orders to lock all the doors to prevent passengers from returning."

"This is my stateroom, right here. I have to get something important. I shall be one minute. Let me pass."

"Sir! Sir! I have my orders," the steward said, trying to block his path.

"To hell with your orders," replied Harry as he pushed him aside and entered his room.

Harry closed his door with his back and tried to deal with the night's madness.

The room relieved some of the pain of saying good-bye to his mother and the horrors that seemed to intensify with each passing minute. It was all so unreal. The ship now sounded as if she herself was moaning in pain as her death was approaching. People were screaming and calling for each other. The outside world was in mayhem. For a few moments, at least, he could feel peace and tranquility.

As he surveyed his surroundings, he had a feeling that someone had been inside his cabin. One door to his armoire was open and also two drawers. His neatly arranged clothes had been disordered. He walked over to get his long, dark, wool coat with a silk fringe at the collar and tossed it over the chair adjacent to the armoire. As he did so, he noticed a navy-blue peacoat flung over it. Then he knew for sure that there must have been a looter inside his cabin.

At that moment the lights flickered, and his attention was drawn to water that was lapping his washbasin. His bottle of cologne reflected the list of the ship's bow. He felt inside the pocket in his tuxedo and took out his Bacon, which he had been carrying with him all evening. He went to his nightstand drawer, took out a silk, monogrammed handkerchief, and carefully folded the book within it. He scanned the room and took a shaky breath. The Louis XIV Quinze clock on the mantel struck two o'clock. Time was running out. The end seemed near. Objects began falling off the furniture, and it was an effort to stand upright.

Reality set in, and he wanted to get back to his father. He needed paternal comfort. Hastily he grabbed the coat from the chair and made his way back on deck, pushing past throngs of panic-stricken people running without direction. Suddenly he saw his father.

"Father! Father!" he called, running toward him.

"Oh God! You're back, my son. Thank God," his father said, embracing him.

The band of eight musicians continued to perform to the bitter end. It was believed that Wallace Hartley, the bandleader, age just twenty-four, strapped his leather luggage case around him and placed his rosewood violin inside it.

Archibald Gracie recalled Clarence Moore, Frank Millett, and Archibald Butt sitting in the smoking room, feigning nonchalance, and that was the last he saw of them. Clarence Moore died at the side of his friend and hero, Archibald Butt. They remained together while lowering women and children into the lifeboats, and jumped when the boilers of the giant ship burst.

George and Harry Widener, together with Robert Williams Daniel, age twenty-seven, a Philadelphia banker, were among those who jumped at the last minute. The three of them went down together. Robert Daniel struck out and lashed at the water with his arms. He was later picked up by passing lifeboat 7.

Harry looked at his father as they jumped into the dark abyss. He became completely submerged, subjected to what was described by others who survived as "a thousand knives being driven into his body."

As his body tried to preserve its temperature by shutting down from the extremities, his fingers, toes, then hands and feet became numb, making it impossible for him to hold on to any piece of debris or furniture he found. His legs wouldn't kick. The wool coat weighed him down and didn't afford any protection from the icy water. He tried to muster all his strength, knowing that extreme shivering and the slowing of his pulse would soon result in loss of consciousness and death.

He looked around at the bodies bobbing in the blackness—the swells like play toys of the waves, their life jackets like white specks frozen in the cold North Atlantic, which seemed to keep them afloat long enough for them to freeze to death.

He heard the dismal cries and moans from the people calling for help, which faded as the people lapsed into unconsciousness and death. Then came the silence.

Some people had a calm and peaceful look, and it was difficult to realize that they were dead. Others appeared to have put up a fierce struggle, as their faces were distorted. One woman came up to the surface close to him, holding her dead child.

He felt shock and disbelief as he turned his head and saw a gamut of images like a flickering horror cinema—incomprehensible. The world order had gone. The sanity became madness.

The physical agony of the icy water and the mental pain caused by the knowledge that, as he could not locate his father, he therefore must have perished, paralyzed Harry's imagination.

Suddenly, all disappeared. As he tried to escape from reality, his thoughts turned to his beloved mother who had satisfied his thirst for book collecting; his library at his home at Lynnewood Hall; his father, whose wealth had enabled him to fuel his obsession as a bibliophile; his brother and sister and his friends from Harvard University. His whole life played itself out before his eyes. He made one final effort to clutch his book—his little Bacon—which he had placed in the inside pocket of the wool coat.

Once of privilege, at this moment I am truly equal to humanity. Fate surely is the great equalizer.

CHAPTER 12
THE AUCTION

October 9, 2011
Washington, DC/Halifax, Nova Scotia

It was a pleasant autumn day, and the trees in the garden were just changing color. Alexei and Annice had separated for a month after they returned from their troublesome trip to Viareggio and England in the late summer. Annice had become increasingly agitated with Alexei, who continued to eulogize about HEW and 223. She took the opportunity to go to Florida to visit her aged mother, who had been ill for some time with leukemia and was now receiving palliative care. A short prognosis was expected.

As usual on a Sunday morning, Alexei took a cup of coffee in his library and read through the *Washington Post*. Suddenly his heart skipped a beat as he read the headline to an article: "Inaugural Sale of Books, Prints, Posters from the Estate of Dr. Jonathan Paul McKeebler, Bibliophile, Principal Surgeon Embalmer on the *Mackay-Bennett*."

Alexei pondered and then presupposed that this was the same Dr. McKeebler who had classified the *Titanic* remains, including body 223, on the *Mackay-Bennett*. Both he and HEW had been bibliophiles, so there had to be something there to help him in his quest to recover the missing Bacon, which he thought might prove the identity of the body in grave 223.

He recalled the well-documented statement that HEW was supposed to have made to Quaritch on his visit to London: "I think I'll take that little Bacon with me in my pocket, and if I am shipwrecked, it will go with me."

Filled with curious excitement, he continued to read aloud to himself. "This is a unique book collection offering clients a wonderful opportunity to admire the wealth of first and second editions. Auction: Wednesday, October 12, 11:00 a.m. Preview: Tuesday, October 11, from 11:00 a.m. to 5:00 p.m. Location: 1685 Young Street, Halifax, Nova Scotia. The following items will be auctioned: books on books; history and topography; wide collection of art books, literature, poetry, and bibliophilic editions. More than one hundred special antique books and manuscripts. Private unpublished edition, *Memoirs from the* Mackay-Bennett, by J. P. McKeebler."

No sooner had he finished reading the notice then he made a manic dash, quickly threw a few clothes together, and hurried to Dulles Airport to purchase his ticket to Halifax Stanfield International Airport.

On arrival, he took a shuttle to the Waverley Inn, an unfussy hotel in the center of downtown. He could hardly wait for the following day to attend the preview. He hoped and prayed that the Bacon would be among the books to be auctioned. On the other hand, if it was, it would have been listed in the advertisement as a book of special importance. Maybe, just maybe there might be a clue in the *Memoirs*?

Alexei made his way to Young Street. He passed George Wright's stately home on the corner of Young and Inglis. His footsteps quickened as he approached 1685 Young Street. The Victorian house was in an impressive Queen Anne style—a large, single-family residence of the type usually erected by prosperous bankers and businessmen. It had the characteristic conical tower, projecting bays, stained-glass windows, and patterned siding. Alexei was enthralled with the regal architectural details and intricate fretwork.

Not to be hindered from his mission, he ascended the few steps to the decorated gingerbread porch and passed the large Entrance to Sale sign. The representatives from Sotheby's greeted him, and a kindly looking, bespectacled lady in her late sixties, who seemed to blend in with the Victorian surroundings, gave him a copy of the catalog. He fervently leafed through it, hoping for a clue. He noticed that the book items were rather more depleted than he had anticipated.

"Are these *all* of Dr. McKeebler's books?" he inquired. "Surely this is not the complete library? What happened to the rest of his collection?"

"No, you're correct," the bespectacled lady replied. She removed her glasses, letting them hang from her neck on a gold-and-pearl chain. "This is only *part* of his collection. A year before his death, he sent a number of books to the Harvard University Library."

To Alexei, that was like a bolt of lightning hitting the rod. He now knew that there was a connection. "When was that? What year?" he asked anxiously.

"Dr. McKeebler died in 1932, but the books to which you refer were dispatched in April 1931. The library here has remained the same since that time. His son married and moved to England, and his daughter married a lawyer and moved to the States." As she exhaustively went through the family lineage in its historical context, Alexei switched off and made polite ahs, ohs, and reallys intermittently. She continued enthusiastically, as if reading from a prescribed text. "After her husband died, she returned to Halifax and raised her children in this house. They were not particularly interested in the books but thought the library was aesthetically pleasing. Now they have all moved away, so, sadly, it is the end of an era for the McKeebler clan with the sale of the estate and its contents."

"Well, thank you for taking the time to share this with me," he said, trying to extricate himself from her and move toward the front door. "I shall take a closer look at the books and possibly come back tomorrow."

With a lump in his throat and a worn-out heart, Alexei returned to his hotel. There were still no leads on the whereabouts of the Bacon. All he had seen of any possible interest was the unpublished, leather-bound copy of *Memoirs from the* Mackay-Bennett by J. P. McKeebler himself. Maybe that would provide something relevant and insightful.

The next day he returned to the house for the auction. The bids for the books were extremely competitive and high prices were paid. The time came for lot 129, the last one of the collection—*Memoirs from the* Mackay-Bennett. A well-dressed, silver-haired gentleman in a dark suit, in his late sixties and speaking with an English accent, started the bidding at eight hundred dollars. Alexei raised him one hundred dollars on each bid until he heard the words from the auctioneer, "Going, going, gone. Sold to number 21 for fifteen hundred dollars," and the familiar, satisfying sound of the gavel on the podium desk. It was his. It was of little encouragement to his quest, but a somewhat secondary connection with McKeebler, the *Mackay-Bennett*, and the embalmed victim in grave 223.

After dinner at his hotel, Alexei spent most of the night reading the *Memoirs* and looking for some kind of clue. If only he could find proof of the whereabouts of the Bacon, then it would all be over. He read and analyzed every word and phrase meticulously, hoping to find some evidence, lead, direction, or sign—but to no avail. He found two itemized memoranda of the identification procedures of the bodies numbered 45 and 223, which McKeebler had recorded at the end of his shift on April 24.

Alexei began to read:

> Name: Edward Herbert Keeping—Valet to George Dunton Widener
>
> Body # 45.
>
> Male.
>
> Estimated age: 32
>
> Hair: Light
>
> Clothing: Grey overcoat marked EK on inside pocket. Black suit, striped shirt, black boots.
>
> Effects: Gold watch and chain; pocket book with diamond and ruby tie pin; cigarette case; keys; lucky cent; 3 shillings and 3 pence in coins.
>
> Paris Address: Ritz Hotel.

"Valet to George Dunton Widener," Alexei mused. "Then the record of 223. I wonder why he recorded those particular bodies in such detail, out of the three hundred or so other bodies. I wonder."

Thursday, October 13, 2011

It was unseasonably chilly for autumn, and Alexei returned to Washington early the next morning feeling very downhearted. He was thoroughly depressed and almost ready to give up. He went through his mail and played back his telephone messages. There was one from Annice. She was going to be in town for the weekend, staying with friends, and wondered whether he would be free for dinner on Saturday.

I wonder why she wants to meet me? he thought. *I wonder whether she is having second thoughts after the month's separation.*

He was apprehensive and anxious about the tenuous situation between them. With trepidation he called her number.

"Hi, Annice. Great to hear from you. How have you been?"

"Good, thank you. I'm meeting some friends for drinks and hors d'oeuvres at the Chevy Chase Country Club on Saturday and wondered whether you would care to join me there around six thirty. Then we could go for dinner afterward."

Alexei hesitated. He never had much in common with her friends and colleagues and had avoided socializing at the club in the past, but on this occasion he thought he could tolerate half an hour with them.

"That'll work I guess. Yes, thank you. So how you are doing? How's your mom?"

"Not much change. It looks bleak. I'll fill you in when I see you."

"Okay. Look forward it. See you there. Bye!"

Alexei hung up with even more reticence and misgivings about meeting Annice.

Saturday, October 15, 2011

Alexei arrived at the white Greek Revival clubhouse. He was greeted by the doorman and was surprised at the heavy security.

"May I help you, sir?" inquired a doorman.

"Yes. I am meeting my wife, Annice Dante."

"Ah yes. Please go straight through, sir," he replied as he pointed him toward the large, eighteenth-century Regency drawing room. It was furnished with Chippendale armchairs and camelback sofas in an array of pastel colors, arranged in a rectangle around the focal point—a white mantel fireplace.

A huge fresh flower arrangement, duplicating the color scheme of the room, was on a circular table in the center underneath a magnificent crystal chandelier.

Annice and her friends were all in conversation while she sat on her own with her back to the fireplace, appearing to hold court.

Suddenly she caught sight of Alexei.

"Alexei! Here you are. Come and join us," she said as she stood up and greeted him.

As he circulated, shook hands, and embraced, he made polite conversation. One or two asked, "What are you working on now?"

When Alexei mentioned the subject of his latest novel and the connection with the *Titanic*, one of Annice's friends asked, "Is he in your story?" pointing toward a portrait above the fireplace.

Alexei paused. "Who?"

"The portrait behind you."

Alexei turned.

"Clarence Bloomfield Moore. You know, one of the three Washingtonians traveling in first class who perished on the *Titanic*."

"Ah yes, of course. Now I remember. I had forgotten the connection between Clarence and the club."

"Most people only know of him due to the speculation as to whether the hounds that he purchased in England went down with him on the ship! Anyway, he was one of the best-known sportsmen in America and was master of hounds of the Chevy Chase Hunt. Unfortunately his death spelled the demise of the hunt, which finally disbanded in 1916."

"I had no idea that he was so revered," replied Alexei in amazement. "Now I know! How very fascinating!"

"Before you leave, take a look in the next corridor, as there are some newspaper and other articles about Clarence and the country club that you might find interesting."

"Thank you. I will," replied Alexei. "In fact I'll take a quick peek now before dinner!"

As Annice began to say farewell to her friends, Alexei excused himself from the company in the pretence of visiting the restroom. He turned in to the corridor and looked at the display of framed photographs on the wall. Arranged on a ledge opposite were albums of the history of the club.

As Alexei was perusing the albums, he came across a copy of a report in the *Washington Herald* dated Thursday, April 18, 1912, which said, "I think I am safe in saying that Mr. Moore had more to do with the development of Chevy Chase than any other man. It was as the result of his efforts that the Chevy Chase Hunt became known throughout the country and that the eyes of the society people of Washington were turned toward the suburb, which afterward took the name of Chevy Chase."

Alexei turned over the page to find another article with a black-and-white photograph of Clarence on horseback. "Clarence Moore was the most daring horseman I have ever seen, and yet one could not call him reckless. He knew every phase of foxhunting, which was his greatest hobby."

Alexei returned to the drawing room and took a long look at the picture above the fireplace. It was a full-length portrait of Clarence dressed in a scarlet hunt coat with a black collar bearing the buttons of the Chevy Chase Hunt and wearing black boots over his camel-colored jodhpurs. He was holding a riding crop in his left hand and was leaning against a stack of large stones.

Just at that moment Annice came up behind him. "What's so fascinating about the portrait?" she inquired.

"I didn't realize that this was one of the passengers who was playing cards with Harry in the smoking room just before the ship went down. He was also at the dinner party."

"So the evening is beginning with HEW, is it?" she said, seemingly upset and slightly irritated.

Her comment was disregarded.

The maître d' diverted what might have developed into a fraught conversation by informing Annice that her table was ready. It had been a month since Alexei had seen Annice, and it was good to see her again. He was optimistic that the night might provide the opportunity to put a spark back into their relationship.

They sat down at a circular table by the window with splendid views over the manicured grounds and the golf course. Alexei was still captivated by her sparkling blue eyes and how the evening sunlight captured the highlights in her hair after all these years.

"How's your research going with HEW and 223?" she asked ambiguously as she fidgeted with her wineglass.

Alexei became suspicious as, all of a sudden, she shifted from being agitated by the connection with Clarence Moore and the *Titanic* to apparently wanting to share an interest.

He was unaware that she had posed the question as a barometer in the expectation that something might have changed and his obsession might have abated. However, after half an hour of listening to him expound, she soon learned that he had become even more obsessive.

"You paid fifteen hundred dollars for McKeebler's *Memoirs* that so far haven't provided any further clues?" she burst out. "That's outrageous! What a waste!"

Annice became red-faced and tight-lipped. "For well over a year you've been consumed by this Harry Elkins Widener and grave 223, but now it's become an unreasonable preoccupation. It's all going nowhere," she retorted in an agitated tone. "You're possessed! And what's more, you're losing perspective. I told you all this when we were in Viareggio in August, and you disregarded my comments and feelings then. I'll ask you again: Where do I fit into all this?"

"Ah," he sighed, "so this is all about you? Is that why you asked to meet me tonight?" His disposition suddenly changed. "Do you want to deprive me of my creativity?" he asked angrily. "You should know me well enough to recognize that that would be my death sentence. You knew who I was when you agreed to marry me. I've not changed."

Annice stood her ground. "Yes, you have. You have become selfish and thoughtless and completely incapable of focusing on anything else. You eat, sleep, and breathe your obsession. Alexei, I'm telling you now that if this marriage is to work in the future, then I should be given equal footing and not have to take second place to some unidentified dead body from nearly a century ago. It might as well be one of your mistresses," she said bitterly as she took another sip of wine. "So what's your answer?"

"And you're so unblemished?" he retorted. "How dare you make such allegations? Can you honestly say that you have had no 'indiscretions' since your illness? You were always away in Europe or somewhere. *Your* obsession was your work—you forgot? So what right have you to judge me? At least my relationships haven't been either physical or emotional for years.

"I'll answer your question with my question," he said as he perked up. "What's happened to the unconditional love and support you once promised to show me? Shallow words, Annice. Your declarations are worthless unless backed up by your actions. I cannot take any more of your demands. The subject is concluded," he declaimed as he threw his napkin on the table in frustration. Now he was anxious to conclude the evening as soon as possible.

"Waiter, the check, please," he quietly and politely requested as he took out his wallet. He continued, "You want an answer, Annice? The decision has been made for us, and the future has been shaped. I am saddened that it had to be this way. Believe it or not, I had hoped that we could rekindle or salvage our marriage." He stood up. "This is not the pleasant evening I had anticipated."

"Nor I," replied Annice quietly as she put her purse over her shoulder. "I had hoped that we could come to some sort of mutual understanding, especially as I am leaving for Europe again tomorrow."

"You're leaving tomorrow? So soon?"

"Yes. I have a three-month contract which will take me to London, Paris, and Rome. At least it will give you the chance to reflect on the possibility that after all these years, our relationship has run its course. Tell me you'll think about it? Otherwise, what alternative will we have other than to contact our lawyers?"

"Yes, of course. But …" Alexei was rather taken aback by the sudden ultimatum. That was something he had not expected. His voice mellowed. "Has it really come to this?"

"Good night then," she said, not giving him the courtesy of a reply.

"G-good night and good luck," he stuttered in a bewildered state.

"And thank you for dinner. I wish I could have said that it was a pleasure," she quipped, half regretting that she had not diffused the conversation before it had turned ugly.

They left the restaurant and went their separate ways again.

Alexei returned home feeling frustrated, angry, and embittered. He poured himself a large cognac, lit up a cigar, and flopped into his armchair. He sat staring at the table for a while, poured himself another drink, and glared at the *Memoirs*. "My life's a disappointment. Annice is a disappointment as well as a cruel bitch. And as for you—you are the biggest disappointment of all!" he shouted at the *Memoirs*.

He swept the book off the table. It was almost surreal as he watched the book glide along the waxed hardwood floor until it came to a stop against the ball-and-claw leg of his mahogany Chippendale secretary.

In his dazed, inebriated state, he thought he saw something protruding from the binding of the book. He crawled toward the book on his knees, still clutching the glass of cognac, which was now dripping all over the floor. He opened the *Memoirs* to the nameplate and caught sight of a small, linen pocket memo book that had emerged from the frail fabric.

"And what have we here?" he inquired in a garbled voice as he picked it up from the floor, pleasantly surprised. "This might be interesting. Let's see, shall we?"

With that, his head fell onto the book and he passed out.

CHAPTER 13

THE DISCOVERY

October 16, 2011
Washington, DC

The piercing, yapping sound of the neighbor's dogs awakened Alexei. He lifted himself from the cold wooden floor. "Oh, what a fricking headache!" he moaned, clutching his head. "Where the hell am I? What happened?"

He dragged himself into the kitchen and made himself his usual double espresso. He picked up the *Memoirs* and the pocket memo book, placed the *Memoirs* on the table, opened up the memo book, and looked through the neatly handwritten pages. As he scrutinized them more carefully, he observed that they were a series of entries, like a personal record. Suddenly he was shaken into sobriety and began to read.

> A fine April spring day with warm sunshine. Nothing to challenge the tranquility.
>
> Routine activities—cut lawn, walked the dog. Took children to grandparents for a few days.

Late dinner with Madeleine. Nightcap.

Library to check auction catalogues for first editions.

Strange, inexplicable feeling of anxiety before retiring to bed.

Dreamt of the identification procedure of body 223, one of the last of the day on the *M-B*. My hand gliding along the silk lining under the heavy weight of the peacoat toward the bulge in the inside pocket. As I did so, I felt a firm, chilled hand on my wrist, as if to impede me from reaching the pocket.

I awoke, trembling, my heart pounding. This was all too vivid and seemed so familiar.

Madeleine calmed me, assuring me that it was just a bad dream.

As I continued to mull over the dream, I remembered that it was a repetition of the dream that I had on the *M-B* a year ago. The only difference was that the cool, damp hand now felt chilled and had moved from pressing on my fingers to sliding across the back of my hand, finally clasping at my wrist.

A R

"What in the world is all this about?" Alexei muttered. He continued to read.

Pain in my hand from the arthritis today.

Madeleine spent the day with friends. Took a walk. Cold and damp in the morning and heavy rain in afternoon.

Spent most of the early evening in the library cataloguing the new books from the January auction.

April and spring again and another year has passed following the horror of the events in the aftermath of the sinking of the great ship. My last day on the *M-B* seems to be foremost in my mind at this time.

Feelings of trepidation. Suddenly very tired. Nightcap then to bed.

Woke up abruptly in a cold sweat, apparently shouting. That dream again—I was on the *M-B*, with my hand gliding toward the inside pocket of the sailor's peacoat, and then the frigidity of that restraining hand now clasping tighter on my forearm that I began to flinch. In horror I awakened to see the imprint of four white fingers on my forearm. I shall look back at last year's entry. Is this something portentous?

Madeleine is so worried and I cannot confide in her.

P M

Alexei continued to scan the pages, looking for some clue. He was so engrossed that he was oblivious that it was now three o'clock in the afternoon. "Damn it, McKeebler, I can't work out what this is all about," he said in frustration as he turned another page.

> Rained heavily today Another year has passed. I feel a sense of impending gloom. A definite feeling of misgiving.
>
> So very tired. The library and my books do not give me peace today. Cannot concentrate. Took out my favorite, unorthodox possession from the safe.
>
> Late dinner followed by a large nightcap in the hope of a good night's sleep.
>
> Made an excuse to sleep in the spare room—am now becoming fearful of the hand. Tried to stay awake but drifted off and awoke just in time to stop the ice-cold hand forcibly restraining my shoulders so that my hand became paralyzed and could not reach the bulge in the pocket.
>
> Beginning to think the contents of that pocket has something to do with this perpetual nightmare
>
> R S

Alexei made a specific guilt connection for the entries. "You're reaching for the book, aren't you? The theft of the book and your guilt has created your demons of revenge." He continued reading:

I decided to read through the last entries to try to find some semblance of rationale behind this recurring dream.

Still the ice-cold hand firmly restraining me.

This is tortuous. From today the journal entries will be focused on the dream and the hand and duly recorded.

Dreading the night. Dream was the same as last year.

I T

April again. Lifeless and languid today. Received a long letter from Rev. Gerard Hood—brought back unwelcome memories. Cannot believe it is five years since the sinking and the time we spent on the *M-B*. The horror and dread of the daily toil of picking up bodies and going through the identification procedures and the embalming and then, for him, the grim task of committing the bodies to the deep.

I don't think that last night on board and the body of 223 will ever stop haunting me.

L I

April has crept up on me again. The recurring dream—my hand gliding along the lining of the peacoat toward the book in the pocket. This time the hand of the body of 223 placed so much pressure with its powerful, freezing, iceberg-like grip around my neck, adhering to it through extreme cold, that I jolted awake, gasping for breath, asphyxiated. My very heart seemed to slow its palpitating beat from the frigid current.

I became paralyzed with fear as I realized that it was my own hand around my neck, strangling, constricting my breathing.

I now know what is subliminally being communicated. I now understand what I have to do.

The feelings of remorse, reprehensibility, and mortification overwhelm me. Has this guiltiness forced me to try to be my own executioner?

A T

It was now four o'clock in the morning. What with the hour, the alcohol, the ordeal of the night's activities, and subsequently the discoveries, Alexei passed out.

***

The morning sun's warm, bright rays shining in his face awoke him from his inebriated state. He washed and dressed and returned to his library to mull over the contents of the memoirs again. "I get over one hurdle and then another presents itself," he mumbled. "I don't know how much more I can take."

Months passed and there were still no leads.

CHAPTER 14

VISIT TO PHILADELPHIA

April 13, 2012
Philadelphia, Pennsylvania

Alexei decided to go and visit friends in Swarthmore for the weekend. He planned to see two exhibits to celebrate the *Titanic* centenary—one at Widener University and the other at the Rosenbach Museum. He was optimistic that the break would help him put the contents of the journal out of his mind temporarily.

He left Washington very early and felt more relaxed after listening to his favorite music while taking in the lovely Maryland countryside during his two-hour drive to Swarthmore. He had a quick cup of coffee with his friends and then made his way to the art gallery at Widener University in Chester, about a ten-minute drive away, to visit "RMS *Titanic:* 100 Years," an exhibition produced and organized by a resident professor emeritus who was an expert on the Widener family.

The university campus was set in a sparse landscape. The architecture was mostly large, white buildings, from a domed mid-nineteenth-century style to the present day.

As he entered the exhibit, he picked up a facsimile of a White Star boarding pass from the table at the entrance. The pass contained personal information such as the name and class of either a passenger or a member of the crew on the *Titanic.* The notion was that at the end of the visit, he would learn whether the person for whom he had a pass had perished or survived the tragedy. He looked at the card. It was Harry Elkins Widener's card. It was another constant reminder of his pursuit. "Come on, Harry. Give me a break," he gasped incredulously. "I've got your card. Don't worry. I'm not quitting on you! That's why I am here."

He looked at the card again. "This is bizarre!" he exclaimed. "No one will believe this."

Alexei pulled himself together and continued with his visit.

It was a small exhibit—not so overwhelming that it could not easily be absorbed. It was set up in small, cubicle-like rooms and focused mainly on the Widener family; the family residence at Lynnewood Hall in Elkins Park; their summer residence at Miramar in Newport, Rhode Island; and people from the Delaware Valley. There was a portrait gallery of *Titanic* passengers from the Philadelphia area as well as a small number of noteworthy people from New York.

The well-known story of the *Titanic* was repeated, but Alexei found the original newspapers from the time interesting, as well as the small-scale model of lifeboat 4, the last to be launched, which Eleanor Elkins Widener, her maid Amalie Gieger, and her friends Lucille Carter, Emily Ryerson, Florence Thayer, and Madeleine Astor had boarded. He also gained a little more information on the identification procedures for the bodies, which he could use in search of answers to the *Memoirs* and 223.

He walked back to his car, still reflecting on the circumstance of the boarding pass. Out of all the passengers and crew on board, how and why did he get Harry's? Was this just coincidence?

One time, he and Annice had visited the Benjamin Franklin Institute in Philadelphia for another exhibit, and they had been given similar passes. Annice received Millvina Dean's boarding card. Millvina was only seven weeks old, the youngest and last survivor of the disaster. Her mother, Ellie, and brother, Bertram, also survived, but her father perished. Millvina enjoyed celebrity status all her life and was invited to open several *Titanic* exhibits, including one in Greenwich, England, in 1994 that Annice had attended.

Alexei had met Millvina in August 1997 during a transatlantic crossing on the *Queen Elizabeth* 2 with his *Titanic* organization. The ship duplicated the route of the *Titanic* from Southampton to New York via Cobh, except that the shipping lanes had been moved south since the disaster. At a champagne reception given in Millvina's honor, everyone had the opportunity of talking with her and asking her questions—of which there were many.

A gentle, sweet-spirited lady with thick glasses, she answered the questions agreeably, but her responses were always prefaced by, "My mother said …"

Alexei had taken the book, *A Night to Remember*, by Walter Lord, to the reception and asked Millvina to sign her name against her entry in the index of passengers. She was delighted to do so but suddenly became agitated when she saw her name. Alexei was concerned. "That's *not* my name," she said as she took the pen and scored out the name Vera. "My name is *Millvina*!"

She corrected the name, signed the book, and smiled graciously.

The sound of a car horn brought Alexei's thoughts back to the present. He returned to Swarthmore to spend the remainder of the day with his friends. They decided to eat out and made their way to Passyunk Avenue in South Philadelphia, where there were several sidewalk restaurants that made the famous Philadelphia steak sandwiches. The smell of onions and fried steak permeated the air.

The first thing the following morning, Alexei made a quick visit to the Pennsylvania Historical Society in Center City, Philadelphia. The building had a stunning exterior and was originally known as the Patterson Mansion. General Robert Patterson of the Mexican-American War had lived there originally. Alexei went to refine his understanding of book collecting before continuing on to Rosenbach Museum.

The Rosenbach Museum had been founded in 1954 and contained great works of literature and fine and decorative arts. The building was in fact two nineteenth-century townhouses situated on a narrow side street in the heart of the historic Rittenhouse Square neighborhood. The street was lined with sycamore trees whose fallen bark crackled underfoot as Alexei walked. The building reflected an age when great collectors lived among their treasures.

Alexei paused at the foot of the steps and read the sign underneath the Commonwealth of Pennsylvania coat of arms.

> DR. A. S. W. ROSENBACH 1878–1952. Among America's most influential rare book dealers, he helped build many of the nation's great libraries. He and his brother Philip established the Rosenbach Museum and Library to share their personal collection with the public. They lived on this block from 1926–1952.

Alexei ascended the white marble steps and made his way to the second floor into a small exhibit entitled "The Rise of Rosenbach," which told the story of the Wideners and Rosenbachs. He thought that the combination of the museum and the *Titanic* would be educationally stimulating and enjoyable.

Harry was a friend, protégé, and early purchaser from Dr. A. S. W. Rosenbach, who was eight years older than Harry. The Wideners' purchases and commissions drew attention to Rosenbach in auction rooms and attracted the attention of other prominent collectors.

On display were Harry's autograph list of desired books, account cards for members of the Elkins and Widener families, an autograph postcard to A. S. W. Rosenbach, and two telegram carbons from Philip Rosenbach. The first was to his brother, dated April 16, 1912:

> WITH 2 DAYS BIDS. NO FURTHER NEWS
> OF HEW OR G.
> MRS AND MAID SAFE.
> TELEPHONE 12 TOMORROW.

The second was to Bernard Quaritch:

> HARRY WIDENER AND FATHER LOST.
> TITANIC. MRS SAVED.
> ROSENBACH.

Another case caught his eye. It displayed Quaritch's letter to A. S. W. Rosenbach dated April 26, 1912, which Alexei found rather poignant and conformant to his search:

> Thanks for the report for the 1st day of sale.
>
> Very sad about the Wideners. I saw that some of the bodies were being recovered so I cabled Philip that Harry had the second edition of Bacon's *Essaies* which he told me he was to keep in his pocket.

> I thought that possibly this might be useful for identification.

The commentary read, "By the time that this eulogy letter was published later in 1912 by Dr. R. the Bacon had become a symbol of Harry's bibliophilic devotion." In Harry's pocket, the book would have had a chance of rescue too.

However, the most crucial and exciting item on display was Harry's manuscript catalog in his own hand, which recorded 368 volumes in his collection and the codified prices paid for his books. Alexei looked at the example and read, "*Some College Memories* by R. L. Stevenson. Edinburgh. For the Members of the University Committee 1886." It was book number 223.

The number jumped right out at him. Why had the exhibitors chosen 223? Of all the books! Why? In images like a movie in fast forward, he recalled all the number 223 connections: the grave site, the first day in the HEW Memorial Library at Harvard University, the discovery here at the Rosenbach Museum.

Like many collectors, Harry had used a ten-letter code word with no repetition of letters for recording the amount he had paid for purchasing his books. He had chosen:

M I N E R A L O G Y
1 2 3 4 5 6 7 8 9 0

He had also added *x* as a second zero, such that xy or yx = 00

The price he had paid for book 223 was coded "a r y x," or sixty-five dollars.

Suddenly Alexei recalled some unrelated letters at the bottom right-hand corners of the entries in Dr. McKeebler's journal. Until now he had given them no thought and dismissed them as irrelevant. What did all this mean?

"Damn it!" he exclaimed. "I bet McKeebler's journal is in code. Why didn't I bring it?"

Alexei skirted over the remaining cases on his way out of the exhibit, displays that were mainly concerned with the Harry Elkins Widener Memorial Library. He was anxious to get home and try to figure out if there was a code in McKeebler's journal. But the final case caught his attention. It was an autographed letter from Eleanor Widener to A. S. W. Rosenbach, dated July 1914. Two years after the sinking, she had slowed down her purchasing and was looking forward to the completion of the library-building project.

> When the Library is finished I want all the books installed there. Then I will feel happiness to know that I have done as my dear boy wished. Over two years have gone since I lost him, & I am no more reconciled than I was at first, & never will be again.
>
> All joy of living left me on April 15, 1912.

The last line reverberated in his mind and moved Alexei close to tears. He felt a genuine connection with her. He felt that she was grateful to him as he tried to find Harry's grave and continue her legacy of completing his library. One book was still absent—his "little Bacon." Somehow he felt that it would ease her burden if they were both found, and she would rest in peace.

Seeing those words, he felt sure that Eleanor Elkins Widener had fully empathized with Emily Ryerson from Philadelphia, on the death of her son, Arthur Junior. He was a graduate of Yale University and was killed in an automobile crash. Emily also wanted to withdraw from the world, and remained in her stateroom throughout the voyage on the *Titanic.*

With the words still echoing in his mind—"All the joy of living left me on April 15"—Alexei left the museum in silent reverence, walked into nearby Rittenhouse Square, sat on a seat, and reflected on recent happenings.

He fought back the tears as he remembered his own mother's pain at the loss of his twin brother, Ethan, who had died in a motorcycle accident when he was the same age as Harry. The nightly screaming and crying, unnoticed and unheard by the rest of the family. She could never explain how she felt. Only a mother could understand and experience the horrific pain and emptiness that lasted a lifetime.

"Parents don't expect to outlive their own children. It goes against what we perceive to be the natural order of life. It is a loss of the future, of hopes, dreams," she used to say as she tried to suppress her tears. "It is an unbelievable journey of grief, loss, and mystery—sometimes anger. It's just so unfair, so unfair."

People used to tell her that time would heal the pain, but it never did for her. The ache remained deep inside her heart. All that was left was a photograph, a frozen piece of time, to remind her of when he was alive.

Alexei recalled Eleanor Elkins Widener's letter to Flora Livingston, wife of Luther Livingston, written in 1914: "I cannot stay long away from the Library. I feel nearer to my boy when I am there."

The haunting painting of Harry by Gabriel Ferrier that hung above the fireplace in the library was equally alluring, so he could now understand Mrs. Widener's sentiments.

He left the park and, on passing the local church, observed that the doors were open. He went inside and sat down. He noticed that the framed paintings of the Stations of the Cross were placed around the church. They represented the journey that Jesus made with the cross on his shoulders, to die on Calvary. The paintings were far larger and more prominent than in his own church at home.

He and his mother, and also Annice, used to follow the "Way" every Good Friday. Today he was sitting just under the painting of the thirteenth station, where Jesus is taken down from the cross and placed in the arms of his mother. She was shown tenderly holding him close to her, not unlike Michelangelo's *Piéta* in St. Peter's Basilica in Rome.

A door slamming and squeaky footsteps interrupted his reflections as the priest came through the door of the sacristy to lock up. Alexei left quietly, proceeded to his car, and, with a heavy heart, returned to Washington.

CHAPTER 15

BREAKING THE CODE

April 13, 2012
Washington, DC

Alexei arrived in Washington in the early evening and went straight to his library to look at McKeebler's *Memoirs* in search of some evidence of a code. He started to scan the bottom right-hand corner of each entry, where he had previously noticed random letters.

He turned to the first entry. There were two letters at the bottom adjacent to one another: *A* and *R*. He turned over to the second entry and found the letters *P* and *M*. *Did he write this in the afternoon?* Alexei wondered. Again, there were two more letters after the third entry: *R* and *S*. Eagerly he flipped through all the entries, and sure enough, every page had two letters. *I* and *T*, then *L* and *I*. This series continued throughout the journal. He was beginning to think that there was something more to this, but was it a code? He could hardly contain himself as he continued to decipher the letters.

With his index finger, he lined up each letter to see if he could make some sense of order and organization. He took the first two, *A* and *R*, and slowly bent up each right-hand corner. The letters on the left-hand side revealed the word *APRIL*. *But what about April?*

he thought. *What does that mean? Maybe the right-hand letters also spell out a word that links with the left.*

He started the same process with the other letters: *R M S T I T A N C.*

"Yes! Yes!" he shouted, not looking at all the letters. "It's *Titanic*! It's *Titanic*!" Suddenly he looked again. "But wait a minute, there's a letter missing. Where's the *I* for the nineteenth entry?"

He went through the pages again and found that there was also the letter *I* missing from APRIL on the left-hand side of the nineteenth entry. Yet again, he examined the pages. There was no tear, no fold. To an average reader of the journal, there was nothing missing.

"Just a moment," he said as he reviewed the penultimate entry. "Recurring dream … book in the pocket … freezing hand around his throat … paralyzed with fear … 'I now understand what I have to do' …"

He stared at the entry in frustration. "*What* do you have to do, McKeebler? What are these 'feelings of remorse'? Where is this page? Why is it missing? Come on; give me some help here."

He read the final entry: "This is the first night that I have not been terrorized by the hand. Have I finally appeased my demons and made retribution for my guilt? The separation from my beloved, cursed possession has given me peace at last."

Alexei thought, L *and* C. *The final letters. What has given you peace, McKeebler? What is this cursed and beloved possession?*

On complete observation he suddenly noticed that one corner of the page was slightly askew. He slowly put his thumb on the corner and with the other thumb began to lift and separate it very, very slightly.

"Here they are!" he exclaimed. "This is the page with the missing letters: *I* and *I*. I had already deduced that you had used APRIL as your code, especially as the disaster took place in April. But why did you need to use a code? Are you hiding something? Did something happen on the *Mackay-Bennett*?"

Alexei was excited as he began reading the missing page. It was the only page to be dated and signed, and the only page to be written on onionskin paper, which accounted for the adhesion.

> Halifax, April 1931
>
> This could be my last entry as my prospect to live much longer has been thwarted by the diagnosis of terminal cancer.
>
> It is hard to believe that next year will be twenty years since the tragedy of the RMS *Titanic.*
>
> This has been a horrendous year. My dear wife, Madeleine, passed away in January. I have not seen my children since her funeral. My son relocated to England, and my daughter married a lawyer from Philadelphia and is living there. I am now alone, somewhat handicapped, and have lost the fight to live. This is compounded by the fact that we are in the grip of the great world depression.
>
> It is now time for repentance. In the hope of redemption for my past indiscretions and the horror of the previous night, I wish to free myself from the burden, guilt, and shame I have endured all these years.

The burden that has been so heavy is that I believe I know the true identity of the victim who rests in grave 223 in Fairview Lawn Cemetery here in Halifax. His name is Harry Elkins Widener. More important is the peace of mind I could have given to the Widener family had I not kept the book.

The passion for collecting books that we both shared resulted in my immoral, unethical, and unscrupulous behavior on the *Mackay-Bennett* on April 24, 1912. I took possession of a copy of the rare second edition of Francis Bacon's *Essaies* of 1598 from inside the sailor's peacoat that he was wearing, thereby confusing and forfeiting his identity.

It was only later, when I looked at the silk handkerchief with the initials HEW embroidered in the corner, that I made the connection between the newspaper article concerning the disposal of the first part of the Huth sale in London and the rare edition of Bacon's *Essaies*.

I could never share the possession of the book with anyone because it would have compromised my integrity and violated my professionalism, as well as bringing disgrace to my family. This critically diminished the pleasure and enjoyment of ownership and has been a punishment in itself all this time.

In a feeble attempt to redeem myself, I had originally intended that my collection of rare books would be bequeathed to the Harry Elkins Widener Memorial Library at Harvard University upon my death. However, with the previous night's terrifying dream fresh in my mind, the collection, including a First Folio of Shakespeare, will now be dispatched tomorrow.

Bacon's *Essaies* had to be hidden, and so I have placed the duodecimo book behind the monogrammed McKeebler bookplate in the front cover of the Shakespeare, thereby surreptitiously returning the book to its rightful owner. It is a perfect fit.

My hope is that this will reunite Harry Elkins Widener and his "little Bacon" in his library and give me some consolation and freedom from the culpability and shame.

Sadly, my cowardice does not allow me to divulge information that could lead to his possible identification publicly until after my death.

I pray that Harry's family and God will forgive me once this is revealed.

Dr. John Paul McKeebler, April 1931

II

"So *that's* what the woman at the auction meant when she said you had already sent some of your books to Harvard. Now I understand why. Damn you again, McKeebler. You sent Bacon with those books."

Alexei could hardly contain himself as he read and reread the final entry: "This is the first night that I have not been terrorized by the hand. Have I finally appeased my demons and made retribution for my guilt? The separation from my beloved, cursed possession has given me peace at last."

"So near now, Harry. So near." Alexei sighed as he sat down. "Just one more step."

He hardly slept that night. He was thinking about Bacon and his own upcoming trip to Boston to give a lecture, "Harry Elkins Widener, the Bibliophile," for the convention of his *Titanic* organization, which coincided with the one hundredth anniversary of the sinking and of Harry's untimely death. It now provided the ideal circumstance for him to combine his lecture in Boston with a visit to Harvard University, where he would try to locate the Bacon.

CHAPTER 16

LOCATING THE BOOK AT HARVARD UNIVERSITY

April 16, 2012
Cambridge, Massachusetts

The spring day was overcast and cool with sporadic rain as Alexei made his way to Harvard University and walked up to the Harry Elkins Widener Memorial Library. He glanced at the steps with a brief thought of Annice seated at the bottom on that sunny August day in 2011. He took a deep breath and sighed. The absence of her on this occasion was painful as he realized that he could not share the day of Bacon's discovery.

He made a brief visit to the library and glanced at the red-and-white tulips that had been placed on the desk on behalf of "the grateful people of Philadelphia for the anniversary of his death." He gazed at the portrait of Harry and said gently, "We're almost there, Harry. Soon everyone will know what became of you and where you are today."

The Houghton Library, a redbrick, 1940s Georgian revival structure where special collections were housed, was situated adjacent to the Widener Library—just a short walk across a small, circular garden lined with pink-and-white Japanese cherry trees.

Alexei was greeted by security staff in a circular room that was decorated with a frieze of the names of Shelley and Keats. *Was this another connection?* he thought as he recollected the beach in Viareggio and remembered the lecturer talking with his students. Percy Bysshe Shelley drowned when his schooner sank during a thunderstorm. He had had a copy of John Keats's poems in his jacket pocket. That was when Alexei first realized that both Shelley and Harry had drowned with their most precious possessions.

A few minutes later, a tall, attractive lady with long auburn hair, dressed in a smart gray suit, emerged from one of the offices and escorted him across the hall to the reading room, where the rare books he had requested were ready for his perusal. He was exhilarated at the thought of seeing the books.

The reading room was very bright and illuminated by natural light. Blond oak paneling encompassed it. There were three or four large desks running laterally toward the circulation desk, where two young librarians were responding to the requests of researchers. A working silence filled the room.

The first book that was brought to him was from Harry's collection of books by Robert Louis Stevenson. The librarian carefully removed it from its specially fashioned, black leather case and gently placed the book on foam supports. Alexei put on the white gloves and when he opened the book and saw the familiar bookplate with the name Harry Elkins Widener, he trembled with excitement. He took a deep breath. As he turned the pages, he observed that Harry had made annotations. He was drawn to its past history and to all those who had handled and possessed it. He immediately felt an intellectual and emotional connection and sensed that Harry was conversing with *him*. For Alexei, this gave Harry vitality. He was no longer distant but real, undeniable and alive at that moment.

Alexei was anxious to see an actual Bacon, but he was only able to see a copy subsequently acquired to replace that which went down with Harry. It was beautifully bound in royal-blue leather with gold trim and a diamond-shaped motif on the cover—similar to the one Harry had purchased from Bernard Quaritch in London.

As Alexei carefully leafed through the pages of the slender, light, and delicate volume on the foam support, he felt an inexplicable attraction and warmth.

The final book that he had requested to see was the large 1623 First Folio of Shakespeare. Alexei's heart raced as he held his breath. Did the folio really hold Harry's "little Bacon"?

He slowly opened the book. A shiver went through him. This was the book to which Dr. McKeebler had referred in his confession. He saw the distinctive McKeebler bookplate—the rococo style, intertwined, bronze-colored initials of his monogram, JPM. Alexei paused, apprehensive of what he might discover. He had waited so long for this moment that he could hardly believe this was a reality.

He ran his fingertips over the plate and felt a slight protrusion. Was this truly what he had been searching for—the item to give credence to his theory?

He reached over, took the copy of the Bacon, and gently placed it over the bookplate. It was indeed the exact size, like the foot in the glass slipper. He could see why Harry had loved it and why Dr. McKeebler had taken possession of it. For Alexei, even as a nonbibliophile, it held a hypnotic power. The book was alluring, causing a feeling of endearment and attachment. It was a hallowed possession for a bibliophile. Was this book the end of Alexei's journey? He gave a sigh of relief and felt a sense of tranquility but, at the same time, wondered how he should proceed.

He thought for a while and then asked the librarian if he could speak with the curator. Within a few minutes, she arrived at the reading room and saw that Alexei was shaking. He had broken out into a cold sweat and began wiping his brow with his handkerchief.

After he had sat for a few moments, he stood up. She took him into a room adjoining the reading room, where there were numerous wooden shelves containing books and files. A long table surrounded by chairs, which seemed to be set up for a meeting, was in the center of the room. A photocopier and a telephone were in close proximity. A marble bust of William Shakespeare occupied one corner of the room, while an overgrown plant stood on the opposite side. A small stained-glass window reflected an iridescent light.

"Please take a seat, Dr. Dante. Now, how can I help you?"

"I have documentation from Dr. John Paul McKeebler's *Memoirs* that within the books that he shipped to the library before he died, he camouflaged Harry Elkins Widener's copy of the rare second edition of Bacon's *Essaies* of 1598 behind his bookplate in the First Folio of Shakespeare. I think I have just located it."

Alexei told the curator the whole story. She was spellbound. The documentation that he provided validated his claims of a hidden book within a book. She made several phone calls and then asked Alexei to return in a couple of hours to accompany her to the restoration area.

***

Alexei watched the delicate, fastidious process of the removal of the bookplate, which was similar to a surgical operation. After about half an hour, a wait that put him into a state comparable to an expectant father, he witnessed the Bacon bound in black morocco gilt being carefully exhumed from the bookplate.

The restorer cautiously opened it. There it was: Harry's own bookplate. They all gasped in shock and disbelief. The bookplate graced all the volumes in Harry's collection—a woman reading on a banquette against a circular window seat, a potted topiary on either side, and two cherubs holding up a banner with the name Harry Elkins Widener on it. Was this the proof? Was it over?

Everyone became very animated. The atmosphere in the restoration room was buzzing with excitement at the remarkable new discovery after so many years. The news quickly spread to other departments. Soon the room was full of astounded and elated colleagues eager to see the long-lost treasure thought to be at the bottom of the Atlantic. This discovery was spine tingling and, for a bibliophile, comparable to the unearthing of Tutankhamen's tomb.

Alexei was now physically and emotionally weakened. He stood up, walked toward the door, and shook hands with the curator and the restorer, too overwhelmed by awe, relief, and incredulity to speak.

Alexei returned to the Memorial Library, still overcome with commingled emotions. It had been a long, complex, frustrating, and difficult journey that began simply in Fairview Lawn Cemetery in Halifax over a year before. After the unidentified grave numbered 223 came the journeys to Pennsylvania, Boston, England, and Italy. He had almost achieved his objective and satisfied his obsession, albeit at the cost of losing Annice.

Now he felt the need to talk to Harry.

"I *think* we've found you," he whispered. "We have your precious Bacon. One more step, Harry, and we *will* find you. You'll be reunited with your Bacon."

CHAPTER 17

ALEXEI'S TRIP TO EUROPE

September 4, 2012
London, England

Although Alexei and Annice had been separated for a year, they had remained in close contact after she returned from Europe. Neither of them had contacted their lawyers, as deep down they did not really want a divorce. Annice seemed to be more open to giving the marriage another chance now that Alexei was almost putting closure to HEW.

Their last conversation had left Alexei with some optimism for the future. Annice had told him that before she retired completely, she had one last trip to make to London in September, as a translator for some delicate international negotiations at the American consulate. Alexei had mentioned that, coincidentally, he had arranged to take the *Titanic* Centennial Triptych tour to Europe at the same time to try to finalize the HEW questions. He hinted that it would be wonderful if they could meet in London. Surprisingly, Annice agreed and even suggested that they travel together when she had finished at the consulate.

Alexei looked forward to meeting Annice in London and wondered if maybe the month's tour would answer that pending question: did their marriage have any chance of survival?

Annice spent the day prior to his arrival making special preparations for his visit. She retired to bed filled with nervous impatience. About two o'clock in the morning, she woke up abruptly as if from a dream, sat up, and stared into the dark room. She reminisced about the years that they had been together and focused on the good times—of which there had been many. She pulled her knees close to her chest and thought, *How I love you, Alexei.*

September 5, 2012

Alexei's plane landed at London's Heathrow Airport around ten o'clock in the evening. He was filled with excitement and anticipation. How he had missed her. They had spent little time together since the disastrous dinner eleven months earlier.

As he made his way through the arrivals hall, he could see her clearly, like an impressionist painting—a hazy, indistinguishable background against which the clarity of her being stood out. The joy of seeing her filled him. He longed for her, to smell her sweet scent and feel her arms around him again. His heart raced and he felt butterflies in his stomach. He waved and caught her attention, and she smiled as their eyes met.

"It's so great to see you again," she said as she embraced him, and they kissed.

"And you," he replied.

"How was your flight?"

"Okay, but very tiring," he responded, sounding very weary. "It was fortunate that I had a flight companion for the seven hours, as we had no movie. At least I was given some extra air miles as compensation. I've felt empty without you, and I've missed you so much," he said, pulling her close to him.

"Me too. What about HEW and the novel?" she asked tentatively.

"Not now. This is our time, not HEW's!" he insisted.

"The car is over here," she said, pointing to a silver Renault. "It's Andrew's."

Andrew was a musician by profession and was principal violist in the London Concert Orchestra. He and Annice had met when they were in line for a security check at Schönefeld airport in the former East Berlin. He was tall, with dark eyes and thick, black hair, and would catch the eye of any woman. A security officer had been shouting at him in German, insisting that Andrew hand over his black, wooden viola case, which looked like a small coffin.

"*Das ist verboten*! *Nein*! *Nein*!" the officer shouted as he tried to wrestle the case from him. Neither of them understood the other, and their voices grew more animated and aggressive.

It was at that point that Annice interrupted. Firmly, yet politely and calmly, she spoke to the officer in fluent German. Suddenly the officer clicked his heels, saluted, and quickly pressed the viola case into Andrew's hands.

"Thank you," he said in amazement. "What on earth did you say to him?"

"You don't need to know," she replied, laughing. "He thought your viola case contained an offensive weapon and was going to take it away to detonate it!"

"Some members of the orchestra would agree that when I play, it is an offensive weapon!" He chuckled. "By the way, my name's Andrew, Andrew Milford," he introduced himself. "Are you traveling to London?"

"I'm Annice Jennings, and yes, I am," she replied as they shook hands.

"Can I buy you a coffee as a thank-you? I was just going to get one myself. We have some time before our flight."

She thought for a moment and then hesitantly replied, "Yes, thank you. That would be nice."

That had been forty years ago. Andrew still retained his striking features, but his hair was now graying at the temples and he sported a goatee beard and mustache. Andrew, Annice, and Alexei had become good friends over the years, even though Alexei had always wondered whether Andrew was one of her earlier "indiscretions."

Although Andrew owned a country house in Oxfordshire, where he spent most of his time when the orchestra was not performing in town, he also had a flat in Blackheath near Greenwich in south London. Annice and Alexei stayed there whenever they visited London. "By the way, where is Andrew?" Alexei asked cautiously, secretly hoping that they would be able to spend time alone together.

"He is on a tour of Eastern Europe and won't be back until late September, so we have the place to ourselves."

The conversation during the drive from the airport was very civil and routine. They passed the well-known London sights: Harrods, Marble Arch, Big Ben, the Houses of Parliament, and, after they crossed over Westminster Bridge, the Royal Festival Hall.

Alexei always looked forward to his visits to London. Naturally, as an historian, he was captivated by Greenwich with its Prime Meridian marked out in cobbles in the courtyard of the Royal Observatory and its connection with the English monarchy.

Greenwich had the cachet of a royal residence. Henry VIII was born in Greenwich Palace and also Elizabeth I, who reluctantly put her signature to the death warrant of Mary, Queen of Scots. Blackheath, on the other hand, was a much-sought-after place for its gentler pleasures, especially golf. James I and his courtiers would swing a club on the heath when he intermittently occupied Greenwich Palace.

They arrived at the flat around midnight, and Alexei was surprised to find that Annice had prepared a romantic dinner.

"Sit down and relax, while I make the final preparations for dinner. I know it's late for me, but this time is perfect for you," she said, removing her coat and tossing her keys on the hall table.

"Thank you. I'm beat!"

She walked up to him, hugged him, and whispered, "I am so glad you're here."

"So am I," he replied, returning the hug after placing his luggage on the floor. She poured him a glass of his favorite wine and lit the candles, which flickered as they toasted each other.

"To us."

"Yes, to us!"

They looked at one another and smiled. She gazed at him through the eyes of her younger days. Alexei became visually transformed, back to the time of their first encounter, when she had immediately been drawn to his youthful masculinity, his mellifluous voice, and his large, strong hands. Particularly noticeable was his enigmatic smile. His height and physique seemed attractively balanced and in harmony with his demeanor.

Her thoughts continued to drift back to the first few years of their relationship. She used to quiver with excitement at the thought of him. Her hunger for passion and carnal desire filled her trembling, gentle body.

They usually concluded dinner with a nightcap. Then their physical longing would erupt. Alexei would lift her from her chair and, with his moist and Herculean kisses, they would make their way to the bedroom.

Her delicate body would be filled with tottering craving as he gently placed her on the bed and then descended upon her, his body diminishing the room's light from gray to black, like the moon casting darkness on the sun in celestial eclipse. Her body would feel a featherlike warmth, followed by a burning heat that radiated from him. She yearned for him. His heavy body lunged upon her and her cries of erotic pleasure fueled and enhanced his manic performance. Their primal instinct for lust's gratification had been foremost.

Her reminiscences were suddenly interrupted by the sound of Alexei's voice.

"Annice! Annice! Where are you? You're not with me. What are you thinking? Is something wrong?"

"Sorry," Annice replied as she was propelled back to the present time and place. "No, nothing is wrong. Really. I was just thinking of the dinners we had years ago and how much tonight reminds me of when we were so happy together."

The evening passed with light conversation. They both seemed to tread softly. "Nothing will soil this evening's reconciliation," she said in a hushed tone as she sensitively took his hand and led him into the bedroom.

September 6, 2012

The following morning, the brilliant early sun awakened Alexei. He turned over, but Annice was not at his side. He sat up, stretched, and called her name, but there was no reply. He wandered toward the kitchen and saw that she had left a note on the dining room table saying that she had gone into the village to buy a few things for breakfast.

He dressed quickly and decided to take his morning walk before the rain came. He turned the corner from the flat, walked through the village, and a few minutes later could feel the cool air of the heath. He loved the village-like feel of the place with its quaint stores, eighteenth-century eclectic architecture, and diverse restaurants.

As he walked, the morning became cool and overcast. His thoughts returned to HEW. Another walk in his footsteps was about to begin. Alexei vowed to make a positive effort to control his obsession for fear that it would set Annice off.

He returned to the flat to find that Annice had made a great effort to make his favorite breakfast, comprising a smoked-salmon bagel, complete with thick cream cheese, tomato, and lettuce, with plenty of garlic and pepper. For old times' sake, she had also made him a special welcome mimosa. They seemed to be on course for an enjoyable vacation together as they gazed at one another in silence.

CHAPTER 18

THE FIRST PORT OF CALL

September 7, 2012
Belfast, Northern Ireland

Alexei was still suffering from jet lag, so the day was spent leisurely making preparations for their trip to Belfast the following day. Both of them had visited Belfast many years before; Alexei with his *Titanic* group in 1994, and Annice in 1980 at the height of the troubles there.

After checking in to their hotel in Victoria Street, they had a quick bite to eat and made their way to the Harland and Wolff shipyard, the birthplace of the *Titanic* and her sister ships, and where Edward Harland and his assistant Gustav Wolff had gained a reputation for constructing high-quality ships. It became the biggest and most productive shipyard in the world.

Much had changed during the last twenty years. The place that was once a deserted shipyard of rusted girders and vacant structures was now vibrant and alive. The area had taken on the title of the Titanic Quarter. Upscale condos afforded views over the River Lagan and a panorama of the rebirth of Belfast since the end of the troubles, with its convention centers, malls, and posh boutiques.

They walked from the hotel through the city. They crossed a bridge with black lampposts and sculptured sea life at the base that resembled the type of bridge one would find over the Thames. The first surviving relic of the *Titanic* they encountered was the *Nomadic,* one of White Star's tenders, in the Hamilton dry dock. The Wideners, among others, had been transferred on such tenders from the quayside in Cherbourg to the great ship anchored in the outer harbor. The *Nomadic* had been retired from maritime duties in 1968 to become a floating restaurant on the Seine in Paris. In 2006, the Northern Ireland government was persuaded to buy it and restore the vessel to its former glory. *Nomadic* had arrived piggyback on a marine transportation barge from Le Havre in 2006.

Alexei stood in silence and just stared at the vessel. He seemed to be transported to that moment in time when the small craft was collecting its first-class passengers and their luggage. *Nomadic* was made from steel with ornate joinery and had four working decks, divided into first- and second-class areas. The Wideners, as well as Benjamin Guggenheim and Cosmo and Lady Duff Gordon, among others, had traveled in the fore area of the deck. A small area in the aft end of the lower deck had been assigned to the overspill of third-class passengers from the *Traffic.*

Inside were cushioned benches, tables, porcelain water fountains, and a buffet bar. It even had separate toilets for men and women. All in all, it was more luxurious than most tenders of the day. This was the sole remaining structural connection to HEW's fatal journey.

Black-and-white photos shot through his mind: those pictures of the Astors and their dog making their way along the pier, and the late nineteenth-century Victorian architectural designs of the terminal.

"I am losing you," Annice said as her warm hand clapped his.

"Well …" He sighed. "Seeing this close up, I feel so connected and so transported to that time. Come on; let's make our way to the plaza." He hurried her across the road.

The exhibit "Titanic Belfast" first opened on March 31, 2012, marking the centenary year of the launching of the legendary liner. *Titanic* belonged to Belfast, which gave *Titanic* to the world, and, after years of guilt and shame, the city had been able to welcome the world to Belfast.

As they approached, they were greeted with a large sign seven feet tall and thirty feet long. The entry sign was cut from the same one-inch steel plate used to construct the ship. Two large crystal-like structures, reaching five stories high, emulated the ship's height, towering like ships' bows in front of them. They passed Thompson Graving Dock, the site of slips 2 and 3, where *Olympic*, *Titanic*, and *Britannic* were built. Alexei felt as if he were in between the *Titanic* and the *Olympic* hulls as they rested on the old ship slipways.

They walked through the stunning central atrium to the galleries inside, which were stacked like deck plans. Long lines of escalators took them to the fifth and sixth floors, where the measureless utilization of glass made maximum use of the vantage point high above the slipways and afforded a panoramic view of the city.

Alexei just stood and gazed in awe at the slipway into Belfast Lough, where *Titanic* had been launched on May 31, 1911. His mind was filled with thoughts of HEW and the other 2,223 passengers and crew who were to embark on her maiden voyage in April of the following year. Annice left him to his reflections and stood by his side in silence.

Suddenly he turned as if snapping out of a trance. "Look at this advertisement," he said as he pointed to the large Afternoon Tea sign. "Let's take a break and enjoy afternoon tea in the duplicated 'opulent surroundings.' We'll see another replica staircase from the ship! I wonder what it'll be like?"

"Good idea," Annice enthused. "There has been a great deal to take in, and my brain is addled."

They were led to a table and given a glass of RMS *Titanic*'s official champagne before the waiters served tea.

"Wow! This is breathtaking. Look at that staircase with its oak woodwork and golden ormolu trim." Alexei gasped as he looked around the suite.

Refreshed, they went down to the plaza, Titanic Place, and were fascinated by the symbolism. There was a map of the northern hemisphere picked out in the pavement. Markers plotted *Titanic*'s course, retracing the fateful journey. There was a halo of dot- and dash-shaped benches around the building that signaled the famous CQD and the SOS distress calls, together with *Titanic*'s own call sign, DE MGY.

Each ship was identified by a three-letter call sign. The DE meant "from" or "this is." CQD was the emergency calling of Marconi operators. SOS was introduced as an international distress call in 1908 and both CQD and SOS were used on April 14.

Trees shaded the benches, and there were a few people sitting in contemplation. The reflective pools alluded to the naval architecture.

With a final look at the *Nomadic*, they made their way back to the hotel.

That evening, they dined at the hotel. Alexei was determined to focus solely on Annice, as he had spent the entire day on all things *Titanic*. There were no leads or anything new to add to the mystery of HEW. Annice was taken by his sincerity and consideration to her.

The hotel was once an old seed house and had been given a second life as a converted hotel. It was conveniently situated just a short walk from the center of the city and also from the Titanic

Quarter. The interior designers of the hotel worked in black and white, from the seating to the walls to the decorative pieces. The rustic restaurant adhered to the black-and-white theme, exemplified by large, heavy wooden tables with white tablecloths, black napkins, and glittering silverware. The high ceilings had been retained from the warehouse days, enhancing the atmosphere. Only absent was the echoing sound of machinery and activities in the granary.

When they arrived at the restaurant the waiter escorted them to where Alexei had reserved a quiet, secluded table in the corner.

"This is so nice," commented Annice as she looked around the restaurant.

"I'm glad you like it," he replied, smiling.

"Alexei, thank you for today and for being so considerate and attentive," she said, looking into his eyes.

"And thank you for being patient with me! I hope you enjoyed the *Titanic* experience as much as I. It felt so good to be able to share it with you."

She leaned across the table and took his hand. "I love you," she said.

They spent the evening talking about all the good times in their past. There was no talk about HEW. They just focused on themselves. They seemed to be so compatible and contented together when there was neither distraction nor petty jealousy. Like the cliché, "the pair of gloves that fit."

"I love you too," he said as he broke a piece of bread and then drank from his wineglass. "To our future," he said. As he toasted her, he bent over and kissed her.

The thrill took her back to those early days when they were the focal points of each others' lives. She could feel the excitement that only he could arouse in her.

With the conclusion of dinner, they took a short stroll through the city. On returning to the room, they felt that it would be a night filled with magic.

CHAPTER 19

THE PILGRIMAGE CONTINUES

September 9, 2012
Southampton via Highclere Castle, England

Alexei and Annice returned to London, and the next place on their *Titanic* centennial pilgrimage was Southampton. *Titanic* had left Belfast on April 2, 1912, and steamed down the Irish Sea, arriving in Southampton on April 4, where she spent a week preparing for her maiden voyage. She had tied up in the extended berth 44, White Star Dock, where she awaited the arrival of the boat trains carrying 930 passengers who had traveled from Waterloo Station in London to the new passenger terminal in Southampton on April 10. At midday on April 12, *Titanic* cast off.

On the way to Southampton, Alexei and Annice stopped at Highclere Castle in Newbury Berkshire, the home of the Earls of Carnarvon for over three hundred years. It had been described as the finest occupied Victorian mansion in England. Alexei thought it was good for the both of them to get a break from all things *Titanic*. Alexei was thrilled that the castle was the set for the popular *Downton Abbey* PBS series, which had taken the world by storm.

As they reached the grand house, Alexei commented, "This reminds me of the Houses of Parliament in London."

"Well observed, Alexei! It certainly is the same architect," Annice answered. She leafed through the Highclere brochure. "It says here that Sir Charles Barry was a preeminent architect of his time."

"No *Titanic* though," he grunted with a smirk on his face, teasing her.

"Not so, Alexei. How could have you forgotten? That's how the series unfolded—the heir to Downton Abbey was lost on the ship!"

"Hell! How did I forget that?"

"I didn't know that it was the fifth earl of Carnarvon who financed Howard Carter's expedition to Egypt's Valley of the Kings when he discovered the tomb of the Egyptian boy pharaoh, Tutankhamen, in 1922," Annice remarked. "It says here that the eighth earl and countess have opened a new Egyptian exhibit in the cellars of the castle."

"Excellent. We can visit when we have taken the tour of the house."

The September day was bright and cool, and the drive along the paved, dusty road drew them close to entrance to the house.

"England is always lovely in the autumn, isn't it?" Alexei observed.

"Yes, it is. Almost comparable with the East Coast."

They spent several hours touring the great house. Annice was pleased that Alexei's attention had been diverted from *Titanic* and HEW. He was enticed by the splendor of the eclectic architecture and interior design. Meanwhile, Annice's focus was on a desk and chair, which came from Napoleon Bonaparte's rooms at the palace of Fontainebleu.

"That was remarkable. Thanks for this wonderful deviation," she said as she took his hand, pulled him close, and kissed him.

Alexei paused. "Oh! You're welcome. But I have a surprise, Annice! Come with me to the gardens, and let's look at a great view of the house. I'd like to take some pictures."

He took her hand. They made their way to the rear of the house to a secluded spot in the gardens, far from the crowds and tourists. The luscious green lawns that had replaced the original orchard and yew arches created focal points. Roses and lavender surrounded the lawn. A gate led to a secret garden—a curvaceous English herbaceous border. It was as if they were lost in an Edwardian fantasy.

Within a few minutes, a lady and gentleman dressed in period attire approached them. "Sir, your afternoon tea awaits you and your lady," the gentleman announced as he led them to a table covered with a white linen cloth with lace designs. "Your waiter will be with you in a moment."

"Oh, Alexei! This is wonderful," Annice said as he pulled her chair out for her.

"Yes, isn't it? Quintessentially English!" he replied in his practiced English accent that always amused her.

Soon the table was filled with a three-tiered plate. The top tier had a selection of tiny finger sandwiches made with cucumber, goat's cheese and watercress, egg, and salmon. All the crusts had been removed, and the sandwiches were triangular in shape.

The second tier had two warm raisin scones with individual portions of Cornish clotted cream and strawberry preserve.

Finally, there was a selection of homemade cakes, shortbread, and canapés—crystallized, edible flowers and chocolate mint truffles.

Their choice of tea was a pot of English Afternoon Tea for two—although Alexei would have preferred Earl Grey. It was served in English bone china cups, and there was a small jug of milk on the side.

"Milk?" asked Annice.

"Yes, you know. It's an English thing. By the way, the milk goes in first to prevent the hot tea from cracking the bone china cups, and you stir it clockwise!"

"What quaint customs!"

Alexei took her every move and action into account as the light autumn breeze touched her fine golden hair.

"Oh, this reminds me of when I was little girl and played that I was having a tea party with my dolls," she said animatedly.

He could visualize her as a sweet little girl and smiled to himself. "It makes me so happy that you are enjoying the day. Shall we take a quick look at the Egyptian exhibit before we leave? We can still be in Southampton before it gets too dark."

The exhibition told the story of the fifth earl's life from the late Victorian period to the time, just after the Great War, of his greatest discovery. There were several artifacts and a faithful replica of the death mask of Tutankhamen.

"Alexei!" she burst out. "The curse *is* true. Listen! It says here that rumors had circulated that Tutankhamen was being taken back to Highclere. After many weeks of wrangling with the world's press and media, Carnarvon was exhausted. He returned to Egypt and nicked a mosquito bite while shaving. It became infected, a fever set in, and he died in the Continental Hotel in Cairo. And that's not all," she continued. "At the moment of his death, the lights went out in Cairo and Highclere Castle, and his favorite dog died!"

Alexei had visited the tomb in the Valley of the Kings on his trip to Egypt in 1991. He had even thought of writing an historical novel about the curse.

"Yes, yes." Alexei smirked complaisantly, indulging her superstitions. "Let's get moving now. It's getting late," he urged. He was becoming anxious to reach Southampton, get back to his *Titanic* pilgrimage, and find any connection with HEW.

The same evening Southampton

The people of Southampton were profoundly traumatized by the *Titanic* tragedy. Five hundred and forty-nine of the victims were from the city. There was hardly a person in Southampton who did not know someone who either lost a life or was related to some crewmember. Over six hundred of *Titanic*'s 885-person crew were local.

After dinner, Alexei suggested they go for a short stroll through the city walls, but Annice had a migraine and so declined.

Little did Alexei realize that this short stroll would be so troublesome to him. The hotel was directly opposite berth 44, White Star Dock, and close to the South Western Hotel, where many passengers had stayed before sailing. He passed Canute Chambers, the former White Star offices, where the list of *Titanic*'s missing was poignantly placed on the iron fence during the days following the tragedy.

He walked through the medieval arch into the old town and could not believe the sheer number of memorials in such a short distance. The Post Officers' Memorial to the British and American post office workers who were on board sorting the hundreds of bags of mail. The Musicians' Memorial in St. Mary's Church to the five-piece band under the leadership of Wallace Hartley and the trio who played exclusively in the Café Parisienne. The musicians had combined to play on that last night. Finally he walked to the floodlit memorial to the trimmers, firemen, and greasers: the Engineers' Memorial in East Park.

He stopped at the Grapes Public House in Oxford Street, ordered a beer, and noticed a small plaque. The landlord told him that many of the crew used the pub before embarking on the *Titanic*, and it was fortunate that two of them had had too much to drink and missed the ship.

However, to Alexei, the most evocative was a humble brass memorial plaque attached to a table in St. Joseph's Church which was inscribed: "In memory of the restaurant Staff who were lost in the SS *Titanic* April 15th, 1912. Subscribed by colleagues and friends."

He knew that Luigi Gatti, who ran the à la carte restaurant on the *Olympic* and later on the *Titanic,* had employed thirty-five Italians as attendants, waiters, cooks, and barbers, most of whom were taken from his two Ritz restaurants in London, Gatti Adelphi and Gatti's Strand. He recalled that it was Luigi Gatti with whom Eleanor Widener had consulted over her dinner party for Captain Smith on that fateful night. He hesitated for a while and felt a shiver run through him. Why did this connection always have a disquieting effect on him?

He returned to the hotel and was thankful to find Annice asleep. He was not in the mood for talking. With the astonishment of finding an Italian connection with Gatti, the Wideners, and his own roots, he had become curious about the Italians on board. Alexei recollected that the first grave they had seen with a name on it in Fairview Lawn Cemetery had been that of Luigi Gatti. He was last seen standing alone on the boat deck, wearing a top hat and tuxedo and carrying a small case with a traveling rug over his arm.

The rug hid the teddy bear that had been given to him by his son Vittorio shortly before sailing. The bear was later found on his father's body and returned to the family. Vittorio disembarked from the *Titanic* shortly before departure from Southampton. Nobody knew why.

From talking with the local people in the Grapes, it was clear to Alexei that there was great sorrow in Southampton among the strong

Italian community that existed in Queen's Terrace. What happened to the Italian staff on board was unclear. Alexei had read that they were herded into the second-class saloon until the end, but he had found nothing to corroborate this.

An article he found moving concerned Signor Alfonso Perotti, twenty years old and an assistant waiter. Perotti sent his mother a *Titanic* picture postcard from Southampton on April 6, 1912, on which he wrote,

"Dear mother and brothers, I have been here two days so that I can embark on the ship to go to America. I'll be back at the end of the month. When you write to me, send to this address: Bowling Green Italian House, Southampton. I'm good. Ciao. Ciao."

Feeling saddened with bemused contemplation, Alexei retired to bed quietly, kissed Annice on the forehead, and fell asleep.

The following morning, they visited the SeaCity Museum. This was a general museum that told the story of the people of Southampton, their fascinating lives, and the city's historical connection to the sea. There was a special exhibition area that contained a completely original *Titanic* exhibit entitled "*Titanic* the Legend." This was informative. It took a different perspective, dealing with the effect the tragedy had on ship design, safety, and technological research.

One room had a transparent, interactive map of the city. Visitors could walk through the virtual streets, and as they did so, lights appeared indicating how many people had lost their lives from that area of the city. It was profound and gave an indubitable understanding as to why the whole city of Southampton felt such agony at the time of the tragedy.

However, most interesting to Alexei was the re-creation of a courtroom. Photos of the players in the tragedy were projected on a screen, while actors recited excerpts from the transcript of the British inquiry held in London after the disaster.

CHAPTER 20

IN THE FOOTSTEPS OF HEW

September 11, 2012
London, England

It was another bright morning, unseasonably warm for the time of year, and, like HEW, Alexei had an appointment with one of the staff in the Archives Department of Bernard Quaritch, the antiquarian bookseller in South Audley Street, Mayfair. Since 1847, the firm had been buying and selling rare books and manuscripts. Quaritch was one of the original members of the Antiquarian Booksellers' Association, founded in 1906. It was the oldest professional body of its kind in the world.

Annice thought it would be a good opportunity to visit the West End. She always loved window shopping in the large department stores and specialist shops, such as Selfridge's in Oxford Street. Her favorite store, Liberty's, was nearby on the same street, with its exuberant half-timbered exterior and an interior resembling a vast Tudor palace. They caught an early train and agreed to meet for a late lunch at the Rivoli Bar at the Ritz Hotel in Piccadilly.

Alexei alighted from the train at Waterloo Station to look at the platform that could be seen in Father Brown's photos, from where the boat train departed for Southampton with the *Titanic* passengers.

Alexei was eager to visit the bookstore and felt a thrill at the thought of following in HEW's footsteps to the place where he had collected his "little Bacon."

As he walked up the street, his heart missed a beat when he saw a large sandwich-board street sign pinpointing the entrance. The sign bore a large gold *Q* logo and "Bernard Quaritch Antiquarian Bookseller since 1847" in black-and-gold writing. The late Victorian, earth-tone building with elaborate floral carvings looked more like a private dwelling than a store.

Alexei pressed the buzzer and was welcomed inside by one of the staff. He walked up the narrow, rickety staircase to the second floor and was shown into a large waiting room filled with antiquarian books and catalogs. A circular table was in the middle. It was just as he had imagined it would be—almost like being transported back to the early twentieth century.

On the wall was a gold-framed portrait of Bernard Quaritch himself. He was bald, with a gentle face, deep-set, sunken dark eyes, and a long nose. He had a mustache and beard with hints of gray that flowed to the base of his tie. Alexei paused for a while. Bernard Quaritch now had a face. He felt he was there. He had made the visual introduction and connection to the man himself.

Underneath the portrait were seven red-bound volumes of Bernard Quaritch catalogs. It seemed to be a bibliophile's tabernacle. In fact, it was a sesquicentennial cake!

Katherine, who worked in the archives department and handled a variety of literary papers, had just coedited a book called *Titanic Calling: Wireless Communications during the Great Disaster*. She was pleased to give Alexei all the information available concerning Harry and the Widener family and their procuring of books.

First of all, she brought out a handwritten ledger containing the date, titles, and amount spent on every purchase made by P. A. B.

Widener and HEW. Alexei was eager to see the entry for Bacon's *Essaies.* As she leafed through the ledger, Alexei became anxious. She seemed to be having difficulty finding the entry. His heart sank.

Suddenly she pointed to the pièce de résistance—on page ninety-six, there was a reference to the third day of the November 1911 Huth sale. "Lot 386—Bacon (Lord) *Essaies. Religious Meditations. Places of Pervasion and Dissuasion.* Seene and allowed, black morocco gilt. SECOND EDITION, EVEN RARER THAN THE FIRST for it differed in the orthography having been changed here and there. 'Meditationes Sacrae' however, are given in English instead of Latin."

As Alexei viewed the entry, he became emotional. He thought of Harry's visit to Quaritch on April 1, 1912, to view the books from the Huth sale, make some purchases, and collect Francis Bacon's *Essaies* of 1598.

April 1, 1912

So now Harry was about to say good-bye to his friend Bernard Quaritch, take possession of that rare edition of Bacon's *Essaies* of 1598, and arrange for the disposition of his other purchases to be shipped on the RMS *Carpathia.*

With delicacy he took the book, spellbound and speechless. His eyes were drawn to the book as if it were a religious object or sacred relic. It was duodecimo-size, bound in black morocco gilt, and had a diamond-shaped motif on the front cover.

He read the words on the sleeve, "Bacon's Essaies, London 1598," and could not believe that he was actually holding it in his hand. Harry told Quaritch that he would take it with him as he didn't want to trust it with the other volumes he had bought. He would keep it in the dispatch box with which he always traveled. "I think I'll take that little Bacon with me in my pocket, and if I am shipwrecked it will go with me."

September 11, 2012

Alexei looked again at the entry and saw that there was a handwritten annotation at the side that poignantly read, "Widener lost in the *Titanic*. £200."

He was deeply moved and unable to speak. The words conjured up the mournful thought of Harry jumping into the dark abyss of the freezing Atlantic with his "little Bacon." Undoubtedly there had been last thoughts of his mother, his library at Lynnewood Hall, and his father, all to try to alleviate the excruciating pain.

In the casual conversation which then ensued, Katherine informed him that the original Quaritch bookstore had been on Grafton Street, about ten minutes' walk from the Ritz Hotel in Piccadilly, where Harry stayed. Harry had often lunched with Bernard Quaritch during his time in London in March and April 1912.

Alexei flinched at this newfound information. He was disheartened that he had not located Harry's "Mecca of Bibliophiles." However, after receiving directions, he thanked her profusely for her time. Feeling stirred by the experience, he made his way to the Ritz to make a lunch reservation. He felt compelled to walk from the Ritz to 11 Grafton Street, the former bookstore, as Harry would have done.

As he was talking with the maître d' at the concierge's office, he noticed a letterhead with the monogram of the Ritz. It was exactly as he remembered seeing it on the original postcard written by Harry to Dr. Rosenbach on March 19, 1912, one month before returning on the *Titanic.* It was addressed from the Ritz Hotel, Piccadilly, London W and had the crest and motto The Ritz London in the left-hand corner. Alexei could visualize Harry writing the postcard here.

Alexei recollected reading the legendary story about the Ritz-Carlton in Philadelphia, that had always amused him. The Ritz-Carlton Hotel located at the southeast corner of Broad and Walnut Streets, in Philadelphia was built in 1911 for George D. Widener. Widener decided to build the hotel after his wife was scolded for lighting a cigarette in the Bellevue Stratford Hotel, located directly across Broad Street. In 1912 Widener traveled to Paris to find a chef for the hotel. He perished on the *Titanic* as he made his return voyage; the chef was not on board.

The late morning had become overcast and cool. He crossed over Piccadilly, the busiest, noisiest, and most fashionable street of the five intersections leading from Piccadilly Circus. It was named after the picadils, or ruffs, made by a well-known eighteenth-century tailor. As he turned left into Dover Street, all the extraneous sounds seemed to become muffled and unobtrusive. He could hear his own footsteps reverberating on the pavement and felt a spiritual, ominous presence, as if it were Harry's footsteps walking with him. He even visualized the pristine appearance of an Edwardian gentleman in sophisticated attire that could only be Harry.

He observed the original, early-nineteenth-century Greek Revival townhouses of smoked purple-and-gray brick. They had white trim and large porticos.

He turned right on Grafton Street and was dismayed to find that in place of the original building at number eleven, there was a rectangular, glass-structured contemporary building with a large, neon sign that read "11–15 Grafton Street." The bookstore had been bombed in the Blitz in the Second World War.

Alexei felt a loss. The connection was broken. The footsteps fell silent.

CHAPTER 21

HARRY'S LAST STAY IN EUROPE

September 12, 2012
Paris, France

The Hôtel Ritz was a grand, palatial hotel overlooking the Place Vendôme. It was founded in 1898 by César Ritz, the Swiss hotelier, eight years before the Ritz Hotel in London. It was the first hotel in Europe to provide an en suite bathroom. Alexei could not help but laugh to himself at the legend of Edward VII getting stuck in the bath tub with his lover at the hotel.

Edith Wharton, author of the famous *The Age of Innocence*, preferred the Hôtel de Crillon. The Hôtel Ritz, she wrote in her novel, *The Glimpses of the Moon,* was "where the newly rich but uncultivated Americans stayed with its Louis XVI suites, calling it the Nouveau Luxe."

As Alexei looked at the plaques indicating that the hotel was sold to Mohamed Al-Fayed in 1979, he immediately drew the analogy between Harry and his parents dining in the imperial suite the night before they embarked on the *Titanic*, and Princess Diana of England and Al-Fayed's son, Dodi, who also ate there before their fatal car crash in the Pont de l'Alma underpass in Paris in August 1997. *Did the imperial suite hold a Tutankhamen curse?*

After dinner, Alexei took his evening stroll on the Place Vendôme. He looked across the square and was drawn to a black figure of a gentleman in evening attire near the central column, gracefully and rhythmically smoking a cigarette as if he were conducting. He could not help wondering whether Harry had taken a walk on the evening of April 9, 1912. Was this an apparition?

Before returning to the hotel, Alexei stopped outside number twelve, where Fréderick Chopin had died in 1849 at the age of thirty-nine. He imagined himself back in 1875 when the Palais Garnier opera house opened on the rue de la Paix, and the center of Parisian fashionable life gravitated toward the rue de la Paix and the Place Vendôme.

The following morning they packed their suitcases, had breakfast, and prepared to say their good-byes. Annice was returning to Washington, DC, from Charles de Gaulle Airport, and Alexei was continuing his centennial trip to Cherbourg, the last continental stopover and final terra firma connection with HEW.

"I'm going to miss you," Annice said, hugging him. "We are doing so well with our relationship, and I just can't let it encumber what you need to do in your quest for Harry, the Bacon, and 223. You need to do this on your own. Now, be sure that you focus and don't miss any clues or subliminal messages!" she added lightheartedly.

"Thank you, Annice. You know how much this means to me to have your support." Alexei hesitated, wondering whether he had made the right decision. "I'll miss you too. I don't want to leave you, but I know you are right. This has to be concluded," he said, squeezing her tightly.

Just at that moment, the concierge announced that Annice's cab was waiting. Alexei walked her to the limousine. After she had settled into the rear seat, she rolled down the window and stretched out her hands. He took them in his, and they touched for a few moments in silence.

"I love you," she said as the movement of the car forced them to disengage.

"I love you too. See you in a few days."

As he watched her leave, he knew that he would miss her. He began to feel an emptiness, a void, even though he always felt the warmth of her presence when they were apart. Again his mind reverted to Harry and his parting from his mother. He felt the empathy of separation and the possibility of not seeing her again.

Annice quickly turned her head and took a last glimpse of him before he faded into the crowds in the street. She too felt a sense of loss but, at the same time, a renewed feeling of stability.

Alexei collected his luggage and asked the cabdriver to take him to the Gare St. Lazare by way of 4 rue de Saint Petersburg, as he was keen to see where Edouard Manet had lived. The Gare, with its stone façade and steel-and-glass train sheds built in 1854, had attracted artists during the impressionist period. Many of them lived very close to the station during the 1870s and 1880s.

Alexei gazed at the Second Empire French Renaissance Revival building in front of him. The structural similarities were reminiscent of City Hall in Philadelphia. He speculated as to whether the resemblance had occurred to Harry, as a fellow Philadelphian, when he was there in 1912 to catch his train to Cherbourg.

He stood at the track and looked at the platform with the wrought-iron pillars that held the ceiling of steel girders. It conjured up Monet's painting with the smoke rising to the heavens through the ventilation shafts.

Alexei became distracted by the departure board, which showed that his train would be leaving from platform 14 at 9:20 a.m. It would arrive in Cherbourg at 12:30 p.m.—a journey time of just three hours and ten minutes. The journey for the Wideners from Gare Saint-Lazare to the Transatlantic Railway Terminal in Cherbourg on April 10, 1912 had taken six hours.

After purchasing a coffee, he made his way up the stone staircase to the entrance hall and glanced at the stained-glass-like murals that displayed pictures of the final destination groups from the fourteen platforms, namely Le Havre, Deauville, Dieppe, and Cherbourg. It appeared to Alexei that it was a cathedral to man's industrial might.

Cherbourg was depicted with fishing boats in colors of brown and burnt orange that were reflected in the water. Village houses with tar-black roofs were in the background, leaving the prospective visitor in no doubt that Cherbourg was a city by the sea.

On board he filled the hours entertaining himself with thoughts of Annice. The scenery became blurred as his eyes glazed over. He endeavored to keep his mind occupied by trying to fit together the pieces of the puzzle.

The location of the book had been solved, but now was the question of the grave site. His thoughts drifted between Annice, HEW, and the outside environment—the farmlands and land formations. Small villages slipped by the window and these were interrupted by utility poles that made a rhythmic whooshing sound as the train traveled at speed through the Normandy countryside.

As the train approached the coast, clouds of dark gray descended over the green hills, giving prominence to the flour-white houses on the headland. In the distance was the opaque color of La Manche, the English Channel. An overwhelming sense of an impending finale, a conclusion, and a termination to his affiliation with Harry engulfed him.

CHAPTER 22

FAREWELL TO HARRY

September 14, 2012
Cherbourg, France

Alexei could not contain himself as he arrived at the coastal city of Cherbourg-Octeville, situated in the Manche region of Lower Normandy in northwestern France. The city was the first territory conquered by the Vikings in their ninth-century invasion. They developed Cherbourg as a port.

Alexei carried a pouch with postcards of the city from 1912 to compare with the present. He found the places from which the two tenders, the *Nomadic* and the *Traffic*, ferried passengers, their luggage, and mailbags aboard the transatlantic liners—in particular *Olympic* from 1911 and the *Titanic* in 1912.

In 1907, the White Star Line instituted Southampton as the principal port for transatlantic steamers arriving at and departing from England. This placed the French port of Cherbourg about five hours away at the speed ships traveled at that time.

The port of Cherbourg did not have the full depth to accommodate large steamers, so ships had to anchor out in the Grande Rade and be serviced by company tenders specially constructed by Harland and Wolff. For the *Nomadic*, which could carry up to a thousand first- and second-class passengers, and *Traffic,* which could carry five hundred third-class passengers and was equipped with conveyors for loading mailbags, it was the first and only time they serviced the *Titanic.*

Cherbourg was the largest artificial harbor in the world. It was a colossal creation made from more stone than the Great Pyramid in Egypt and built to resist the violent storms that swept the English Channel. Emperor Napoleon III, Empress Eugénie, and Queen Victoria inaugurated it in 1858. Several forts of defense were built at Cherbourg between 1794 and 1857.

Alexei wasted no time in visiting the special centenary exhibit. Five cities to which the *Titanic*'s story was connected wished to collaborate for the centenary. Alexei was now at the end of his pilgrimage: Belfast, the place of construction; Southampton, port of departure; Cherbourg, the first stopover; Cobh (Queenstown), second and last stopover; Halifax, the place where most of the bodies found offshore were laid to rest. Cherbourg had been the only continental port of call for the *Titanic.*

The exhibit was housed in the Cité de la Mer, the former Cherbourg transatlantic terminal, built in the 1930s art-deco style, now restored and accommodating the museum. It encompassed the site of the baggage hall and original terminal building.

Alexei stood in line, took his boarding pass, and attended the magnificent show. At the end of the exhibit, he would find out whether the person named on his pass had survived the tragedy.

There were two themed sections. The first section guided him through the baggage hall, where interactive displays echoed the hope and excitement of those about to board. He discovered what life would have been like for Harry on board as he walked the length of the reconstructed hull of the vessel, from the luxury suites and grand staircase of the first-class accommodation to the sparse and repressed corridors of the third class.

The eight-foot-long screen that projected a film documenting *Titanic*'s journey, from the crossing to the collision and, finally, the sinking, fascinated Alexei. He was intrigued by how this exhibit exploited film, photography, sound effects, and reconstruction to tell the story and envelop the visitor.

The date and place were charted on the screen and the time line was displayed at the base of the railing. Sounds of the water, the engine, and the communication between the ships in the tapping of Morse code signals accompanied the film. It was all so realistic that Alexei could sense the coldness as the ship approached the iceberg and hear the creaking sounds as the ship slid across it. At 2:20 a.m., when the ship sank, he was transported through a visual illusion below the surface of the sea, accompanied by the pertinent sounds of the water until, in the depths, there was silence.

The final section focused on the investigation into the tragedy.

September 15, 2012

Alexei awoke early and made his way to the transatlantic railway terminal that had once taken passengers to the *Titanic.* The Second Empire–style building had been dismantled in 1933 to accommodate larger liners such as the *Queen Mary.* He walked along the pier and visualized the little fishing boats as tenders. He even saw in his mind's eye the famous picture of the Astors and their Airedale dog, Kitty. He imagined the Wideners and their valet and maid, along with other first-class passengers eagerly awaiting the tenders.

It was Wednesday, April 10, 1912. Harry Elkins Widener, his parents George and Eleanor, Edwin Keeping, the valet, and Amalie

Gieger, Eleanor's maid, left the Gare St. Lazare in Paris at 9:40 a.m. They arrived at the transatlantic railway terminal of the New York express train in Cherbourg six hours later.

At five o'clock, the small White Star steamship the Nomadic *began transferring the first- and second-class passengers and their carefully labeled luggage to the great ship. A second steamship, the* Traffic, *picked up the third-class passengers.*

Finally he returned to the memorial that marked the spot from which *Nomadic* and *Traffic* had departed. He turned and looked down the Port de Plaisance into the Grande Rade near the Fort de l'Ouest and gazed at the bow of a fishing boat, imagining that it was the *Nomadic* and Harry was on board.

That would be the last image Alexei had of Harry. He reached into his jacket and pulled out a copy of the picture of Harry that he had taken at the Memorial Library in Harvard.

I guess this is good-bye, Harry, he thought as he walked away. *My journey with you is concluded. Now I must continue alone.*

CHAPTER 23

THE LAST PORT OF CALL

September 16, 2012
Cobh (Queenstown), Republic of Ireland

Alexei had hoped to take the Celtic Link ferry service from Cherbourg to Rosslare in order to replicate part of the path of the *Titanic* but it would have taken seventeen hours plus another two hours to Cobh. He was eager and impatient to complete the final part of his pilgrimage and return home.

After an early breakfast, Alexei took a cab to Cherbourg train station for his return journey to Gare Saint Lazare in Paris where he transferred to Charles De Gaulle Airport for his short flight to Cork. It was a cold and wet late afternoon when Alexei finally arrived in Cork. He felt completely alone. His connection with HEW was broken; Annice was three thousand miles away in Washington, DC; and, in fact, he wondered why he had made the journey there. He felt the need to call Annice and hoped that he wouldn't reach her voice mail. As he dialed the number, he felt a wave of excitement run through him.

"Hello? Who's this?"

"Annice? Annice?" he repeated, not recognizing her voice. "This is a bad line. Hello, Annice. It's me—Alexei!"

"Alexei? What's up? Where are you? Are you all right?"

"Yes, I'm fine. I'm in southern Ireland—in Cork. It's a long story. I had to take an early train from Cherbourg to Paris and then take the only daily flight from Paris to Cork."

"What on earth are you doing in Cork?" she asked in astonishment.

"Just tying up a few loose ends and putting the final ghosts to rest. Actually I'm waiting for a train to Cobh. It's only half an hour from here."

"Cobh? You're crazy! Why didn't you visit when we were in Belfast instead of traveling back and forth? I don't understand. I thought you were coming home. I'm confused!"

"As always, I have to finish what I started and follow the path of the *Titanic* as far as her departure into the Atlantic Ocean at the beginning of her maiden voyage."

"I thought you had done with HEW and all that. When is this all going to end? What?" She began to get agitated and raised her voice.

Alexei realized that no amount of explaining would either placate or satisfy her. He was in no frame of mind to justify himself, so he handled the truth a little carelessly by interrupting her. "Must dash, the train is coming! Bye. Love you. Take care. See you in a few days." He promptly hung up.

"Bye. I love ..." but the connection was broken, and she didn't finish the sentence.

He had decided to take the train for the short ride to Cobh, as the train would pull into the very same platform it had in 1912. He was pleased to be able to duplicate the exact course many of the *Titanic* passengers had taken, including disembarking at the dockside station. He observed that little had changed, either at the station or in this quaint town, from what appeared in the old photographs he had seen. It was like being in a time warp.

In the departure quay was a statue of Annie Moore, the fifteen-year-old girl who was the first person to be processed at Ellis Island.

He spent a few hours reliving the Queenstown part of the story—the *Lusitania* memorial and the jetty where the *Titanic* passengers boarded the harbor tenders, the *America* and the *Ireland.*

He took a stroll through Promenade Park, which had been renamed Kennedy Park since 1963, and visited the Cobh Heritage Center—the original customs clearance hall for the millions of Irish who emigrated to the United States, Canada, and Australia during the great potato famine. It was interesting to read about the immigrants leaving Ireland. Their amazing story was dramatically presented in a multimedia exhibit in the wonderfully restored Victorian railway station.

The center also housed a *Titanic* display that re-created a section of the ship's deck, where each of those who boarded in Queenstown was identified by name and fate.

Alexei's mind reverted to his visit to Southampton, recalling the grief of that city. He could empathize with the statement that Queenstown was known as the saddest place in Ireland because of the emigrants who left Ireland for North America between 1851 and 1912 and made their last farewells to their families on the quayside.

One hundred and twenty-three passengers embarked on the *Titanic* on April 11. The famous photographer, Father Frank Browne, who was training to become a Jesuit priest, disembarked there, having received a telegram that said, "GET OFF THAT SHIP—PROVINCIAL." His obedience to his superior's orders probably saved his life.

His uncle had given him a ticket for the maiden voyage of the *Titanic* from Southampton to Queenstown, Ireland, via Cherbourg as a gift in April 1912. He had a cabin, A 37, on the promenade deck. He took dozens of photographs of life on board and captured the last known images of passengers and crew, including Captain Smith and Archibald Butt.

He had made a unique record of the early part of *Titanic*'s maiden voyage beginning with passengers arriving at Waterloo Station and boarding the *Titanic Special* and ending with the ship steaming into the open Atlantic.

Alexei made a final sojourn to the same White Star jetty where, on April 11, 1912, passengers were entertained with traditional Irish airs by the uileann piper, Eugene Daly, as they waited for the tender *America* to take them to the *Titanic* at the outer liner anchorage. As Alexei stood there, a piper was playing the famous tune "Erin's Lament."

Although HEW had been on the ship having lunch, probably taking little notice of other passengers as they embarked from the tender, Alexei felt a sense of totality. A dark gray, heavy mist descended on the esplanade, bringing visibility down to less than a hundred yards. Rain teemed down while thunder and lightning reigned in the air.

Titanic sailed to her destiny from Queenstown, and now Alexei was to fly home to his predestination.

CHAPTER 24

ALEXEI'S INCONCLUSIVE JOURNEY

September 20, 2012
London, England/Washington, DC

Alexei returned to London to say good-bye to his friends and take his flight back to Washington, DC. During the eight-hour flight, he read, dozed, and watched a few movies to pass the time. His thoughts were still concerned with the survival of his marriage to Annice and his spiritual journey with HEW. Furthermore he had unanswered questions that troubled him: Would the Widener family come through with a DNA sample to verify the person in grave site 223 in Fairview Lawn Cemetery? Would there be enough DNA for such a sample? Would this provide closure? Was McKeebler's guilt, built on the belief that the book was taken from HEW and not from a sailor, well-founded?

Even now so many questions continued to surface. Would he ever know the truth?

Alexei was anxious to end the flight. He turned to the map channel on the plane's audiovisual system, only to find that the flight simulator located its position over the city of Halifax, Nova Scotia, where the mystery had begun with grave site 223.

The time remaining was two hours and twenty-three minutes—223.

AFTERWORD

This novel is fabricated around historical data that has been meticulously researched before being transformed into this vivid and thought-provoking mystery novel. Fiction and reality are intertwined.

Through historical entertainment, this is an imaginative telling of Harry Elkins Widener, in the hope that an image emerges of his world and the events of April 1912.

Sadly, the real HEW's body was never found. Similarly there is no evidence to suggest that the Bacon was ever recovered.

The author personally followed each stage of the final journey of the *Titanic* from Belfast to Halifax, Nova Scotia. Each destination was visited during the centenary commemorations in 2012 to authenticate the historical and geographical sites.

Historical data were compromised by the quagmire of inaccurate and conflicting information as to whether the Wideners boarded the *Titanic* in Southampton or Cherbourg.

Therefore it became paramount that the author was persuaded to take literary license.

The three main characters, Dr. McKeebler, Alexei, and Annice, are fictitious, as are many of the events.

Similarly, the railings and the paneling at the B&B on the Isle of Wight, U.K., were from the RMS *Aquitania* when she was scrapped in 1950 and not the *Mauretania*.

ACKNOWLEDGMENTS

These individuals were personally consulted, and each place was visited to give the novel credibility.

J. Joseph Edgette, PhD	Emeritus Professor and Emeritus Folklorist, Widener University
Susan Tsiouris, MSLS	Head of Public Services, Wolfgram Memorial Library, Widener University, Chester, PA
Jan Alexander, MA, MS	Reference Librarian and Archivist, Wolfgram Memorial Library, Widener University
Rachel Howarth	Head, Public Services and Curator, Harry Elkins Widener Collection, Harvard University
Elizabeth Fuller	Librarian, Rosenbach Museum and Library, Philadelphia, PA
Lee Arnold	Senior Director of Library and Collections, Rosenbach Museum and Library, Philadelphia, PA

Susan Heim	Assistant Director of Research Services, Rosenbach Museum and Library, Philadelphia, PA
Leslie Morris	Curator of Modern Books and Manuscripts, Harvard University
Research Librarians	Harvard College Library, Cambridge, MA
Ann Mosher	Bibliographic Assistant, Temple University, Philadelphia, PA
Katherine Thorn	Archives Department, Bernard Quaritch, Antiquarian Booksellers, London
Barbara Esstman	Writer/Editor
Ruth Jones	Executive Assistant Manager, The Ritz, London
Georgina Bissenden	Personal Assistant to the Executive Marketing Development Manager, The Ritz, London
Christian Boyens	The Ritz, Paris
Hugh Brewster	Author, President, and Publisher, Whitfield Editions
Chris LaMarca and Staff	Dolley Madison Library, McLean, VA
Sharon Ford	Director, Swarthmore Public Library, PA
Mary Tobin	Assistant Librarian and Head of Information Services, Ridley Township Library, PA

Historical Society of Pennsylvania	Philadelphia, PA
Matthew and Sara	Electric Reads, UK
Titanic Historical Society Inc.	

Helen M. DiFulgo and Dr. Anne Howard for their continual support and encouragement.